The Oxley Crossing Romances
Australian Rural Romance

Finding Mr Wright

LENA WEST

Published by Gymea Publishing

Copyright © 2017 Lena West and Gymea Publishing.

All rights reserved.

No parts of this work may be copied without the author's permission.

https://www.facebook.com/LenaWestAuthor/

www.lenawestauthor.com

ISBN-13: 978-0-6482110-6-8

Disclaimer

This story is a work of fiction.

Names, characters, places and incidents are the product of the author's imagination and are used fictitiously. Any resemblance to events, locales or actual persons, living or dead, is entirely coincidental.

Some actual locations may be referenced in passing.

Table of Contents

Disclaimer iii

Table of Contents iv

Dedication viii

1 1

2 11

3 23

4 27

5 37

6 57

7 71

8 75

9 79

10	95
11	103
12	107
13	127
14	129
15	149
16	161
Epilogue	167
Here is Your Preview of Unto Death	172
About the Author	186
Other Books by Lena West	188
Connect with Lena!	192

FINDING MR WRIGHT

Lena West

Dedication

This novel is dedicated to Marie. Thank you for encouraging me to persevere with my writing.

FINDING MR WRIGHT

1

"Megan! Guess what! I've found Mr Right!"

Her mind still lost in the column of numbers, Megan Armitage, with a glow of contentment converting her ordinary features topped by short mousy hair, to a simple beauty, marked her place with her finger and straightened, putting her other hand to her back to ease her pregnant bulk as she did so.

Excited and happy as she was to be having a baby, her condition was beginning to make the simplest tasks awkward in ways she had never imagined possible. She was counting down the last few weeks till her body would be her own again.

"What?"

Geni Sullivan, her best friend and also her brand-new business partner as from today, uttered a breathless giggle, a blush staining her cheeks beneath her carefully applied make-up.

"You know I'm a dyed-in-the-wool romantic, right?"

In an unconscious gesture Megan was very familiar with, she used her fingers to comb the mane of straight, naturally pale gold hair she'd been too rushed that morning to braid, back from her face.

"I'm always raving on about there being one perfect man, our Mr Right, for each of us? Like your Jon for you?"

Megan nodded, wondering what nonsense Geni was on about now. Her friend was noted for exaggeration and hyperbole where men were concerned. Although…. A puzzling thought sent a frown flickering across her brow.

Geni had been acting strangely unlike her usual exuberant self, ever since her arrival in Oxley Crossing the week before. Quiet and subdued, as Megan had never seen her, and, until now, no mention of her accustomed favourite topic of conversation – men. Or, to be more precise, how to find and recognise the *right* man. Megan had never known anyone so determined to find her Mr Right, in spite of the unfailing disappointment she suffered each time the latest candidate turned out to be, not a prince in disguise, but a mere frog. Or toad, as was sometimes the case. Even now there appeared to be an almost hysterical edge to her upbeat mood.

To tell the truth, Megan was becoming rather concerned about Geni, without any idea of exactly why she should be, so she paid closer attention to the silly conversation than she normally would have.

"Well. This morning when I enrolled Jamie in school, we were waiting in the corridor outside Ms Marsden's office, when the door next to us opened and out stepped that gorgeous hunk I met at your wedding last year."

Geni flicked a self-conscious, sideways glance at Megan.

"You know, tall, moody grey eyes, dark hair silvering at the temples. Looks like he works out regularly."

A grin flitted across Megan's face.

Coupled with the location, she instantly recognised the man Geni described, but she didn't interrupt the flow. This was more like the Geni she knew and loved. Maybe she had simply been feeling stressed over the move, the new job, and settling into a new town. Country life was way different to what her friend was used to in Sydney.

Quietly amused, she listened as Geni rattled on.

"He stepped up to me, hand out as if I was a long-lost friend, and said, 'I remember you. We met at Megan's and Jon's wedding. Jenny, isn't it? I'm Ben Wright, the school principal.' I remembered him too. He made a verrry favourable impression on me, I can tell you. My heart was fluttering so madly I barely heard him, but I latched onto his hand, and like an idiot said, 'Geni Sullivan. Accountant, and mother of Jamie.'."

Geni laughed again, fanning her hand in front of her face.

"I tell you Megan, that man is hot!"

This time it was Megan's turn to laugh, partly with relief that her friend was back to what constituted normal for her, and partly at the new image of the principal of Oxley Crossing Central School which Geni had planted in her mind.

Sure, Ben Wright was an interesting, highly intelligent man. Good-looking even, in a quiet, studious way. Several local women had made unsuccessful plays for him; but she would never have thought to describe him as 'hot'.

Interestingly, the faint blush staining Geni's cheeks deepened as she continued.

"It wasn't until he shook Jamie's hand as well and I heard the kid say, 'Nice to meet you, Mr Wright,' that the name registered. At the wedding, not expecting we'd ever meet again, we were just Ben and Geni. When Jamie and I came here to live I hoped… wondered, I mean, if I'd meet him again. But still, it took me by surprise this morning to run into him when I least expected it."

Geni wandered into the kitchen through the door behind their offices and put the kettle on.

"Just think Megan," she called, only half facetiously, over her shoulder. "His name. He's Mr Wright, although he spells it with a 'W'. I checked the spelling on his nametag, but what a coincidence, eh. Reckon the butterflies in my tum mean he could be 'The One'? *My* Mr Right?"

Megan shook her head, chuckling as she reached for the canister of herbal teas. She sniffed enviously at Geni's coffee, but Junior wasn't allowed caffeine. Which meant she wasn't either. Yet another reason she was counting the weeks.

Geni was unbelievable, but she was her best friend, a friend who was solidly and thoroughly reliable. She'd trust her with her life.

In fact, she was trusting her to take care of the business she'd painstakingly built from scratch, and which came next in her life after family. It had been a case of mutual recognition of kindred spirits since the day they'd found themselves assigned to adjoining desks in the Australian Taxation Office in Sydney, and she was so happy to see her friend acting like herself again.

Although Geni was a couple of years older than herself, they had hit it off immediately; the biggest difference between them being Geni's perpetual search for her 'Mr Right'.

What a turn-up for the books if that elusive gentleman really did prove to be sober, serious Ben Wright. As the idea took hold in Megan's mind, optimistically, she began to think maybe her two friends would be good for each other. Something along the lines of opposites attracting, perhaps. Her smile deepened.

A word in Eddie's ear, maybe…?

Her dearly loved stepmother was acknowledged as Oxley Crossing's most successful matchmaker. A new romance in the offing might distract some of her almost overwhelming attention from Junior. Eddie was acting as if this was the most important baby since the Virgin Birth.

"You never know, Geni," she encouraged, doing her bit for the cause, "love is in the air, or maybe the water, here in The Crossing. First Dad and Eddie, then Jon and I, Angie and Alan, and not so long ago there were whispers on the bush telegraph about Sophie James and Bob Whitman, although nothing came of that. So, who knows? Maybe you and Ben will be next."

Her smile dimmed a little, and all at once she was frowning slightly.

"A word of warning, though, Geni. Ben was married, and by all accounts was deeply in love with his wife. She died. Leukemia, I think. Anyway, it was very tragic, and he was still grieving when he arrived in The Crossing. Be kind to him Geni. Think carefully about his feelings before you get too involved with him."

"Oh, you needn't worry, Megs. I won't be getting involved with anyone. I'm through with men for the foreseeable future. It was just that I was struck by the coincidence of his name."

Before Megan's eyes, it was as if a light had been switched off, leaving her lively, vivacious friend looking lost, and, almost impossible to believe, afraid. Afraid, and... hopeless?

Worry flooded Megan again, stronger than previously. This was so not Geni. Whatever did Geni Sullivan have to be afraid of? Especially since it was Ben Wright, absolutely the most honest and reliable of men, who'd caught her eye. Something was seriously amiss with her friend. It had to be something which had followed her up from Sydney, didn't it?

A client's arrival for his appointment meant she had to set the issue aside for now, but she made a mental note to get to the bottom of the mystery ASAP.

~~~~~

Ben couldn't get back to the safety of his office on the Secondary School side of the Kindergarten to Year Twelve campus fast enough.

That slip of a woman, Geni Sullivan, with her warm green eyes, and sleek, pale blonde hair brushed into a glossy mane reaching half-way down her back, had invaded his mind far too often for comfort since he'd danced with her at the wedding last year.

When he'd heard Megan Armitage, the town's sole accountant, was taking on a partner who was an old friend from her Sydney days, he'd wondered if it could be the same woman who haunted his dreams too often for comfort.

Hope had put an extra spring in his step. Hope that had just been abruptly dashed.

Coming straight from a meeting with his senior staff members, his mind fully occupied by classroom logistics, to find himself face to face with her, had momentarily floored him. Only his well-honed social skills had saved him from making a complete ass of himself in front of the dozen or so curious staff, parents and kids milling around in the foyer.

Even more embarrassing had been getting her name wrong; but when they met at the wedding he'd been so dazzled he hadn't been capable of taking in such irrelevancies as names.

God, I was almost drooling over the woman! he continued to beat himself up. *Then, she went and introduced her son!*

He could still hear her bright, chirping voice when she stated, '... mother of Jamie.'

Mother!

Was that her discreet way of telling me she's married? Had she been warning him off? It was a good thing there was nobody to see his dark scowl.

He was sure she had been, otherwise, why come out with it like that, as if she was making sure he knew she hadn't meant anything by her flirtatiousness at the wedding. That she wasn't looking to continue it here and now. Which was unfortunate; since she was the first woman he'd really noticed in *that* way since he'd begun taking notice again. As out of practice as he was with flirtation and dating games, his lack of confidence now had Ben believing the connection he'd experienced at the wedding was all in his own mind.

While every fibre of his being urged him to make a play for her, his practical common sense dictated the exact opposite. His disturbing sexual awareness of her made him vulnerable. A feeling he wasn't familiar with, and one he didn't like.

There was no way he'd lay himself open to losing the respect of his friends and neighbours in Oxley Crossing by chasing after a married woman.

A married woman who was the mother of one of his students.

~~~~~

Jamie Sullivan, a sunny-natured, tow-haired nine-year-old with a smattering of freckles across his nose, and his mother's green eyes, had pushed aside a bundle of files to perch on the corner of his mother's desk. Legs swinging, he recounted the highlights of his first day at Oxley Crossing Central School in between inhaling chocolate chip cookies and juice.

"... and my teacher is Mrs Johnson. She's old, but she seems pretty cool. Bailey says we're lucky we got her and not Mr Reilly. Bailey says he's a real nark. He sends more kids to detention than any other teacher in the whole school. It feels really odd, you know, Mum. Having high school kids at the same school as us. Although their playground is over the other side of the buildings. We've been teamed up with a year nine class for Peer Support, Mrs Johnson says. I wonder if that means we have to go across to the High School buildings or if they'll come to us?"

His tongue slowed long enough for him to take a much-needed breath, cram another cookie into his mouth, and for his mother to slip a question in edgeways.

"What about that Mr Wright we met this morning? Will you be seeing anything of him?"

"Hardly, Mum. Mr Wright's the principal of the whole school. Ms Marsden is in charge of our part. But Bailey says Mr Wright is coaching the Under Ten cricket team this year, so I might see him there. That's Bailey's team, and he said I can join if I want. Can I, Mum?"

"I don't see why not, although the season's almost over. They may not be taking new registrations, you know. I'll find out about it tomorrow."

"No need. Bailey says he'll take me to training on Wednesday evening across on the Oval. Can I go and play cricket in the park now? Bailey and the others will be waiting for me."

Receiving an affirmative from his mother, he scoffed a last cookie and ran off to join his new mates, leaving Geni gazing fondly after him.

She was glad to know he'd found his feet so quickly, although she had a suspicion she was going to get tired very quickly of hearing her son's every statement prefaced by the magic words, 'Bailey says...'.

All the same, she intended to keep an especially close eye on him until she knew for sure they were safe here in Oxley Crossing. This little, barely-on-the-map town ought to be as safe as it seemed for a while yet.

After that...

There was no way she would let anyone, anyone at all, harm her son. Her fingers curled into tightly clenched fists, and the happy smile disappeared from her face.

Megan would have found this flinty-eyed, pugnacious woman almost unrecognisable as her happy-go-lucky friend.

2

"Hi, I'm Alan Morgan, team manager, and you must be Geni Sullivan, Megan's friend. Are you here to sign young Jamie up? Bailey's already informed me we have a new recruit."

"That's right."

Geni's eyes strayed across the sports field to where Ben Wright had turned to greet Jamie and his new best mate, Bailey Tan.

Seeing her looking his way, Ben gave her a perfunctory wave, then turned aside to address the group of children milling around in the middle of the field.

There was nothing she could put her finger on, but something about his brief, unsmiling greeting had given Geni the feeling she had just been brushed off. A reaction she wasn't accustomed to meeting from the male of the species. Even this Alan Morgan, whom she knew from Megan to be happily married, had given her an appreciative once-over.

Anyway, if Ben Wright really wasn't interested, it would make it easier for her to resist him.

She knew perfectly well she had no right to be interested in him, not with all the vile baggage from her past resurfacing; she just had to get that message through to her unruly hormones. Giving herself a mental shake, she returned her attention to Alan, filling in the registration form he produced.

She was about to sit down and wait till training was over, but Alan pre-empted her.

"No need to hang around, Geni. I'll see Jamie home when we're finished."

About to refuse, she changed her mind. Jamie would hate it if he thought she was babying him, even though she wasn't keeping nearly as close an eye on him as she wished she could. Smiling, she accepted Alan's offer. It was no big deal, since she lived a very short stone's throw away, across the other side of Bridge Street in the flat above the service station.

Just the same, when Jamie came thundering up the steps an hour later, she was sitting on the top step, watching for him. Just as she was making a habit of watching intermittently through the office window when he played in the park after school.

~~~~~

Every cell in his body responded with quivering awareness when Ben glanced up to see Geni Sullivan standing on the sidelines, the low sun setting her pale mane ablaze, her eyes trained on him. He opened his mouth to shout an eager greeting, when he abruptly recalled all the reasons why letting her, and all the world, know how she made him feel was such a bad idea.

He'd invested quite a bit of time, more than such a simple exercise warranted, thinking up a whole catalogue, besides the most obvious one.

Remembering their first meeting, when they had gazed raptly into each other's eyes while slow-waltzing round the dancefloor, he'd even attempted to convince himself she was the worst kind of flirt.

Time that had obviously been wasted.

At that moment he became aware of Jamie and Bailey running towards him. Jamie half-turned, waving to his mother over his shoulder.

Stupid! You stupid damned idiot! Ben silently berated himself.

It wasn't *him* she was watching; it was her son. He hoped none of the kids he ought to be focusing his attention on had noticed the heat he felt scalding his cheeks. His hand was raised in an unconscious gesture, as if reaching out to the woman across the field, and he turned it into a half-hearted wave of acknowledgement, immediately turning his back on her to call the kids to order.

It was a good ten minutes before his eyes strayed into the forbidden direction again, to see her walking away from him. *Thank goodness*. When he realised she wasn't staying, he felt tense shoulder muscles unknot and his breath whoosh out in relief.

A while later he chanced to look up and saw a blur of pale blonde hair on the corner of the narrow veranda at the top of her steps.

Every time he looked again, deliberately now, she was still there. He always encouraged parents to keep tabs on their kids, but this degree of vigilance was surely excessive in a town as safe as Oxley Crossing. Unless he had it all wrong, and she was simply enjoying the fresh evening air after a hot day. He shrugged, and, training over, got on with supervising the kids putting the equipment away.

~~~~~

On Friday night, Megan and Jon insisted both Geni and her son join them at the pub for dinner.

"It's become a bit of a Friday night tradition for quite a few of us, Geni." Megan said. "You'll get to meet the Morgans, and sometimes Elizabeth and Geoff Tan are there as well. You ought to take the opportunity to meet them, as I predict Jamie's going to be spending as much time at their place as Bailey has at yours this week."

An irrefutable argument. She had seen more of Bailey Tan, both before and after school than she had ever seen of any of Jamie's friends in Sydney. The two boys were fast becoming inseparable, and she did want to meet Bailey's parents and assure herself they were comfortable with the situation.

And yes, she admitted to herself, *I do want to vet them to be sure Jamie is safe when he's out of my sight.*

As it turned out, Geni found herself at the centre of a large, convivial group of friends, a number of children among them whom Jamie already knew from school. With the kids settled at their own table, the adults were about to order when Ben Wright wandered into the dining room.

From the ensuing comments, she deduced that, a bachelor, he was a regular, opting for Marge Morris's nourishing, homestyle cooking any time he wanted a good meal he didn't have to prepare for himself.

He was immediately invited to join the party. People shuffled their chairs to make space for one more. Space Geni was disconcerted to discover was next to her, since she was the only other single person present.

She had been trying so hard to squelch her burgeoning interest in him, and the last thing she needed was to have him so close she could smell the tang of his citrusy after-shave with its underlying scent of clean, highly desirable male.

Close enough that she couldn't avoid accidently brushing her arm against his every time either of them moved so much as an inch in their chairs.

Close enough that his rich baritone sounded as if he were whispering in her ear.

Heart racing and mouth suddenly dry, she couldn't for the life of her think of something even half-way intelligent to say.

Swallowing her embarrassment, she hoped to goodness no-one had observed her confusion. She flicked a comprehensive glance round the table, groaning under her breath when Megan caught her eye and dropped one lid in a secret wink.

If Geni was uncomfortable with Ben sitting next to her, it was nothing compared to how he felt.

He was a man to whom 'honour' and 'integrity' were more than mere words, especially in his dealings with women.

Being seated shoulder to shoulder with the only woman in The Crossing with the power to raise his pulse rate higher than an hour in his extremely well-equipped home gym could, he should have been revelling in the opportunity offered to get to know her better.

To impress her with his wit, intelligence and personal attention.

To arouse her to a fever-pitch matching his own with subtle, and not-so-subtle, 'accidental' touches. Caresses.

Unless the woman was taboo. Then it became unbearable torture which he struggled to hide from his well-meaning friends.

All he could do was pretend she didn't impinge in the slightest degree upon his consciousness. Turning slightly sideways to talk to Alan Morgan on his other side, he manfully ignored her. Until she bumped into him while bending to retrieve her phone from her bag to show Elizabeth some photos she had taken of the boys playing with Jon's dog, Trixie, in the backyard.

When Eddie Patterson commanded his attention from the other end of the table, Geni filled his vision as he leaned forward to speak with Eddie. By rare good fortune, Geni was now the one turned away as she continued her conversation with Elizabeth.

So it continued throughout the longest meal Ben could ever remember at 'The Vic'. He barely finished swallowing the last mouthful before he pushed urgently back from the table. Uttering a general farewell along with a muttered excuse about work waiting for him at home, he made his escape.

Thank God he ran a tab and didn't have to hang about waiting to pay for his meal and the single beer he'd choked down.

Unable to settle to anything constructive when he reached home, he ended up pounding the pavement on a late run, hoping to exhaust himself to the point of being able to sleep.

~~~~~

Geni thumped her pillow into shape and tried unsuccessfully to get comfortable.

At this rate, I'll look a positive old hag by morning, she grumbled to herself. Now there was an idea. If she looked as bad as she felt, no-one would wonder at it that Ben had found her forced proximity tonight so unpalatable he'd rushed off before the dessert menu had been consulted. She'd heard a couple of surprised comments.

Apparently, he had a real sweet tooth and never, absolutely never, skipped dessert.

Except tonight he had.

It was me. I know it was.

Swearing off men herself was one thing. Being treated like a pariah by the most attractive man she'd met in forever was entirely another.

Couldn't he at least allow the possibility of a casual friendship?

For Jamie's sake if not hers? In her entire life she had never been so thoroughly snubbed. Rejected.

She sniffled back an unexpected tear. Why did everything seem so awful in the middle of the night?

~~~~~

Nothing was quite as bad in the morning as it had seemed while she tossed and turned, agonising over it in the dead of night. Even the bags under her eyes were easily disguised with a light application of concealer so she looked fresh as the proverbial daisy when she finally surfaced to fix breakfast.

So what, if Ben Bloody Wright found her eminently resistible? She'd already determined she couldn't have him, so she ought to be glad, for his sake, that he wouldn't be getting hurt. Her own pride didn't matter a damn in the long run, even if the wound she'd been dealt did hurt like hell.

The only male she needed to concern herself with was her Jamie. Which reminded her... A glance out the window confirmed what her ears had already told her – Megan and Jon were breakfasting alfresco in their back-garden oasis next door. Calling Jamie to the table, she picked up her coffee and snatched a piece of toast off the plate and headed for the door.

"Back in a minute, Jamie, honey. I just need a word with Megan."

"You haven't forgotten you promised to take Bailey and me for a picnic at Rainbow Falls, have you, since our team has a bye this weekend?" her son asked anxiously.

"Not for one minute. I've already packed the food in the cooler and it'll only take a minute to grab the rest of the gear when Bailey gets here."

It had given her a warm glow, helping Elizabeth Tan by offering to entertain Bailey on what was often the busiest day of the week at her new friend's bakery and café. It meant she belonged. She was trusted.

But first she had to catch Megan and Jon together, before Jon left to open his garage below her flat.

"Megan. Jon. Can you spare a minute?" she asked, not waiting for an answer as she sat down across from them, her half-eaten breakfast in hand. "There's something important I need to ask you both."

"That sounds ominous. How can we help you Geni?" Jon quirked an eyebrow at his wife's best friend.

"It is serious, Jon. As you both know, I'm a single parent, and Jamie means the world to me. He's the main reason I jumped at your partnership offer, Meggie. I wanted a safe, secure place for him to grow up. But I worry what might happen to him if anything happens to me in the next few years while he's still a child."

She turned her mug round and round in her hand, distress showing in the wobble of her tightly compressed lips.

"Nothing's going to happen to you, Geni. You said it yourself; you've come to a safe place, here in The Crossing."

"I do hope so Jon, but there's things... We can't see what the future holds, can we? Anyway, what I'm here for right now is to ask you if you'll agree to be Jamie's guardians if the worst happens. Will you?"

She looked from one to the other of her friends, a hint of desperation in her voice.

Megan reached across the table and clasped Geni's hands in a warm, reassuring grip accompanied by an equally reassuring smile.

"Of course we will, Silly, that goes without saying. You know, we've had this conversation before, Geni Sullivan. My answer is the same now as it was then."

"That was before you went and got yourself married. I'm not taking Jon's consent for granted." She turned to address Jon directly. "Will you promise me to think about it, Jon? Talk it over with Meggie and let me know what you decide."

"No need to think it over, Geni. I'm here for you and Jamie both, whenever, and however, you need me. Right, Megan?"

"Absolutely. So now, Geni, please relax. You've been rather uptight since you arrived. I've been a bit concerned about you. Are you good now?"

Both Jon and Megan noticed that Geni hesitated as if about to say something more, before she nodded briskly and stood to leave.

"I'm good. And thank you both for taking a weight off my mind. I'll let my lawyer know. He'll get it all tied up in red tape so that no-one can interfere with your rights if anything does happen." She walked round the table to give Megan a hug and kiss on the cheek, repeating her actions with Jon. "I'm so blessed to have you for my friends."

As Geni jogged up the stairs to her flat, Megan's eyes followed her, a deep frown creasing her brow.

"That was so weird," she murmured to her husband. "Far from erasing my concern, now I'm more worried than ever."

"Nah. I don't think it's anything to worry over. She's just being sensible about providing for a worst-case scenario. She'll be right."

Megan patted Jon's hand and smiled.

"You're probably right."

Jon was a good man, and she loved him with every fibre of her being. She knew he worried about her with the baby so close, so she didn't say what she really thought. But he didn't know Geni the way she did. In her heart she felt Geni was anticipating that worst-case scenario as something more likely to happen than not. And happen sooner rather than later at that.

FINDING MR WRIGHT

3

The sly bitch gave Kev the slip.

She disappeared from the flat in North Sydney where her and the brat lived, but he'd told his mate, Kev Simpson, to track her down again. Kev was a genius when it came to finding people. Butch had known it would pay off in the future when he'd befriended the miserable little nerd and protected him from the bullies.

First time, Kev had hardly been on the job a couple of days when he'd located her in Sydney, so he ought to be able to find her again just as quick. With so much on-line data available it was harder than most people thought to disappear and not leave a trail someone like Kev could follow, easy as pie.

Butch frowned. Maybe having Kev send her all those notes and the photos he'd told him to take of the kid had been a mistake. At the time he'd written them, planning with Kev to have them delivered, it had seemed a good idea to remind her where she belonged. Who she belonged to. He'd looked on it as an early start on retraining her.

Only, damn-it-all, she'd got the wind up and run, giving poor old Kev the job of tracing her all over again.

Kev reckoned maybe they were only gone on a holiday, but Butch didn't agree. It seemed a funny time for a holiday with school going back and all. He still reckoned they'd done a runner. Scared off by his messages Kev had been dropping in her mailbox. He hadn't counted on that. He'd thought she'd curl up, all scared and paralysed into mute obedience the way she used to when he laid down the law to her.

He shrugged. It was done now and couldn't be changed. But maybe when they located her again he'd tell Kev to lay off. At least till he was free to take charge in person.

On the bright side though, it proved she still took him seriously. His mouth stretched into a wolfish grin as he walked away from the phone, thinking how much he was going to enjoy the obedience training he had all planned out for the bitch. Plans he'd been refining in his mind for years.

As always when he dwelt on those wasted years, Butch felt the rage building up inside of him, and slammed his fist into the brick wall, swearing long and loud at the ensuing pain.

Damn-it-all! She was his wife! They'd been married in church, all right and proper. Joined by God until death. She belonged to him. She'd promised to obey him, only he hadn't had enough time to teach her to respect his rights the way she should.

In the beginning, he'd been too lenient, letting her think she could do what she liked; then he'd had to come the heavy and chastise her more severely than he'd wanted to.

Even then, she'd continued to defy him, running off to the old woman like she had.

When he caught up to her, he'd teach her right this time. She'd learn to obey him; either the easy way or the hard way. He kind of hoped it would be the hard way. He had scores to settle with the bitch. There'd be no more leniency. This time she was going to have to learn to please him, or else.

The longer it took her to learn how it had to be, the worse it would be. For her.

Butch sniggered. The notes had only been the opening salvo of the softening up process.

Yep, he decided. He'd let her think she'd got away, until he was ready to deal with her.

Those early warnings could still be turned to his advantage. Once he appeared on the scene in person, she'd remember them, and they would have a stronger effect then, making his job of training her so much easier. When he finally got his hands on her.

FINDING MR WRIGHT

4

"Have you heard the news?" Megan's step-mother, Eddie Patterson bustled into the office, excitement adding pink roses to her cheeks and a sparkle to her eyes.

Megan and Geni, discussing the day's appointments, looked up.

"Something good, judging by your happy expression."

Eddie did love to be first with the news, though she was no idle gossip. If the matter was confidential, she could set an example to oysters.

"Right you are, Meggie. This is the most exciting thing to happen in ages. Remember that book Angie was writing?"

Megan nodded, a happy grin appearing on her own face as she anticipated the nature of Eddie's news.

"Well, she not only finished it, she's found herself a publisher. She signed the contract just yesterday. Alan's so proud, he's throwing a party to celebrate."

"Wonderful! Just think. Oxley Crossing now has its own resident author."

Just then the phone rang, and Geni went to answer it, leaving the other two discussing Angie's achievement. The next minute she laughed out loud.

"It's Angie for you, Meggie. Congratulations Angie. Eddie's just told us your wonderful news," she added, then held the phone out to Megan.

Megan offered her own congratulations, chatting for a few moments, before calling to the others. "Angie's ringing to invite us all to a BBQ at 'Morgan's Run' on Sunday arvo. Reckons it'll save time, catching three of us with the one call. I've already accepted for us, Eddie. Are you and Jamie free, Geni?"

In no time at all Geni had been persuaded to accept, even though she and the Morgans were such new friends, and Angie had hung up to make the next call on her list.

Back in her own office a little later, waiting for her first client of the day to arrive, Geni wiped away a stray tear trickling down her cheek. It was wonderful to be accepted so easily in her new home town. She could be so happy here, if only... Another tear followed the first before she firmed up her trembling lower lip and stemmed the tide before she really turned on the waterworks.

Steadying her nerves with a caffeine hit, she pulled out the emergency make-up kit from her desk drawer and repaired the damage. Hearing the outer door open for the second time that morning She shoved the cosmetic bag out of sight and conjured up a cheerful, professional smile, silently praying she wouldn't be forced to let Megan down after her amazing generosity.

~~~~~

Another perfect blue-sky summer's day greeted her when Geni looked out the window on Sunday morning, causing her to study the cloudless expanse with a hint of unease. If it didn't rain soon, the town would be put on water restrictions and the crops would shrivel up and die. With the majority of their clients being farmers, she'd heard this concern voiced so often she'd begun to share the countryperson's perennial obsession with the weather. Although, she acknowledged, she had another reason for hoping today was the day the long-anticipated rains would come.

If it poured, she'd have an excuse to leave 'Morgan's Run' early. She had been feeling a slight sense of nausea every time she thought about Angie's celebratory BBQ.

Ever since she'd heard that Ben Wright had mentored Angie when she first began writing. Still did. With that connection, he would be front and centre at the event. While she knew he was unlikely to seek her out, she also knew she was going to be subjected to more than enough of the sight and sound of the man. Her nerves would be stretched to breaking point. She supposed she'd better get used to it. Oxley Crossing was too small a community for a citizen as prominent as Ben Wright to be easily avoided.

As it turned out, she needn't have worried herself into a frazzle. In such a crowd, Ben was no more than a distant figure on her horizon and she was able to relax and lose herself in the music and dancing.

There she was. Ben had hoped that Geni, being so new to town, might have chosen not to come, but no such luck.

Once he'd seen her, it seemed he couldn't rid himself of his awareness of her presence, try as he might. And he did try. He even tried to start up a flirtation with Sue Renski who had been throwing blatant invitations his way ever since she'd split up with her last boyfriend. But even Sue wasn't desperate enough to tolerate his half-hearted efforts for long. Which left him a prey to Old Thommo who bent his ear with apocryphal yarns of the good old days when farmers didn't need a degree in computer science to know how to make a living off the land.

Escaping Thommo's clutches at last, he carelessly let himself get hemmed in at the refreshment table with the woman he was determined to avoid just in front of him, being served with a drink by Alan's teenage cousin who'd been roped in for a stint as barman. Only Rhonda Molinar, whom he judged to have had one or two drinks more than was good for her, separated him from Geni. With people pressing in behind him, the only way to go was with the flow. Two back from Geni Sullivan, being tortured by the sound of her voice as she chatted with Rhonda.

"Soda water! Loosen up, Geni. Give her a wine, Mickey. Geez, this is a party, ya know."

"No thanks, Mickey. I'm driving, and I've had my quota."

"Yeah, okay. That's where I'm lucky," Rhonda conceded. "James is driving tonight. It's his turn as designated driver."

The two women, fresh drinks in hand, moved off slowly. Ben, about to peel off in the opposite direction, was still close on their heels when Rhonda asked a question he had to admit, he was curious about himself.

"Hey Geni. I've been meaning to ask. How much longer till young Jamie's dad joins you in The Crossing?"

Ben slowed his steps, lingering within earshot to hear Geni's answer. Quite sober, unlike Rhonda, what he witnessed aroused even more questions. Geni stopped abruptly, her glass slipping through fingers that seemed to lose their grip, spilling its contents down the front of Rhonda's dress. Even in the dim light outside the woolshed, Ben would swear Geni had lost every last vestige of colour. She swayed, and thinking she was about to faint, he stepped forward to catch her.

Catching sight of him for the first time, Geni glared at him, and, pulling herself together, apologised profusely to Rhonda for the spilt drink. As she contributed her last clean tissue to help mop up, she gave a brief reply to the original question. She'd had a moment to think, and realised if that was what Rhonda was thinking, maybe others were too.

Maybe *Ben* was. He'd certainly noticed her shock at Rhonda's nosy but innocent question and looked as if he might have a few questions of his own given half a chance. He'd had a really peculiar look on his face just now. Better if she scotched any speculation before rumours started spreading.

"You asked about Jamie's dad, Rhonda? Not in the picture. I divorced him when Jamie was just a baby. That's the last we've seen of him, and since that's the way I like it, I hope it stays that way."

"Really?" Rhonda chuckled. "Better watch out for Eddie then, or she'll be setting you up with the first single male you look sideways at. Eddie does love weddings."

Ben, shocked to discover he'd been labouring under such a huge misconception, had been stopped in his tracks as the women moved on.

Bloody Hell!

He should have overcome his scruples and gone snooping in Jamie's enrolment file. He'd have saved himself a ton of grief if he had, only he'd refused to do what he would have given a staff member hell for if he'd caught one of them doing anything of the kind.

So where did that leave him? After the way he'd been giving her the cold shoulder since day one, she'd be well within her rights to slap him down hard if he tried coming on to her now. He took himself off into the dark paddock to sit under an old red gum tree on the creekbank and have a serious think. The billions of stars, twinkling and sparkling in the black void, brighter than they ever did in the city, as if they were additional party decorations, calmed his jangled nerves.

~~~~~

The party was still in full swing half an hour later when Ben marched back into the middle of the action, a determined expression now taking the place of his earlier stunned mullet impersonation. He was looking for Geni, and she wasn't hard to find. Joey Lambert fancied himself as a dancer, and he had the floor, with Geni matching him move for move in what had turned into an exhibition dance.

Ben bided his time, enjoying the spectacle as much as the rest of the appreciative audience. When the music finally stopped he stepped forward with a couple of cold drinks for the performers. As Joey's mates gathered around, clapping him on the back, Ben eased Geni out of the crowd to where hay bales provided seating in a quiet corner. When she made no move to evade him, he decided to chance his luck.

"So, you're a single mum, Geni Sullivan. With such a warm, loving personality I had you pegged as a family woman for sure. Thought your husband was wrapping up work commitments before joining you and Jamie in The Crossing."

He was watching her closely and caught the quick upward flick of her eyes before she lowered them to the can of cola in her hand. She was listening alright, even though she hadn't said anything. Encouraged, he continued.

"Back when I danced with you at the wedding, you knocked me for six. Then you knocked me for six all over again when you arrived in town, only, because of Jamie, I thought you were spoken for, so I backed off."

He caught another of those fleeting upward glances and moved closer. Removing the now empty can from her hands, he stood, tugging her to her feet along with him.

"They're playing a slow song Geni, so how about it? Shall we start again with another waltz in the moonlight, and see where it leads us?"

Still without a word, Geni fell in beside him, turning into his arms when they reached the dancefloor and began circling round and round. She thanked the Lord he had the sense not to chatter on. The way she was feeling, there was no way she was capable of conversation.

Talk about being knocked for six! That's exactly what he did to me tonight! See where a waltz in the moonlight leads us indeed. She didn't know whether to feel affronted by his hide after the way he'd been avoiding her or be encouraged by his admission she'd knocked him for six.

If only...

She scrunched her eyes tight shut to hold back incipient tears. She'd take this waltz as the gift it was, but there could be no more. She didn't think she could afford the way Ben's touch weakened her resolve.

The music slowed to a halt, and Geni stepped back, her hands sliding down Ben's arms, releasing him from their hold.

"Thank you Geni." His soft, deep voice caressed, making her yearn for the impossible. "What say we stick together and dance away what's left of the night. It feels wonderful, holding you in my arms. If I call you tomorrow, will you agree to go out with me? As a couple? I'm not forgetting Jamie, but I'd like to have you to myself the first time."

Finally coming to her senses, Geni raised her head, her eyes meeting his for the first time.

A cold chill skittered down Ben's spine as he took in the deep sadness inherent in her expression. It was only then he recalled her shock at Rhonda's inquiry earlier that night. Was there more to the story than she'd admitted to?

"Ben..." she began her refusal, but then her fighting spirit, which had been sadly absent in recent weeks, kicked in.

She hadn't been entirely joking when she announced to Megan she'd found her Mr Right, and every time she encountered Ben, she became more certain of the depth of her attraction to him.

Now, when he was finally noticing her, she'd be damned if she let him go without fighting for what might be.

"It's good to know you had a decent reason for giving me the brush-off for the last couple of weeks, Ben," she began again, "and I'm glad we can be friends now. But although I like you Ben, friendship is all I have to offer at the moment. I'm not going out with you. Or anyone else, either. I've temporarily given up dating, but if we happen to be in the same place, I'll be more than willing to spend a little time with you."

Her courage wearing dangerously thin, she turned away from the hurt showing clearly on Ben's expressive face.

"Why Geni? I can see you've got something bad going on in your life. Can't you trust me to help you?"

Could she?

She knew she wanted to, then realised that yes, she could. In fact, for Jamie's sake, she was going to have to very soon.

Only tonight was neither the time nor place for explanations. She needed to get her thoughts lined up first, so she didn't sound like some hysterical ninny.

"You're right, Ben, you can help. Now isn't the time, and there are others I need to talk to first, but since it concerns Jamie, I need to talk to you, Mrs Johnson and Ms Marsden. Will you set up an appointment with all three of you for later this week? I don't want to have to repeat my story more often than I have to."

Ben nodded.

"Leave it to me, Geni. I'll let you know." He was going to say more, but she was already hurrying away.

"I have to get Jamie. It's time I took him home."

Her heart quivered inside her breast when she looked back and saw the deep concern Ben made no effort to disguise. He was such a good man. If only the timing was better.

"Goodnight Ben," she called over her shoulder as she hurried off to collect her son from the *Starwars* movie-fest in the room set aside for the kids.

Resisting the urge to run after her, Ben stoically watched Geni walk away from him. He'd let her go. For now. But he was making it his top priority to find out what calamity in Geni Sullivan's past had so traumatised her that she was shutting herself off from any chance of a happy future.

In his profession he'd seen enough broken and dysfunctional families to have his suspicions, but he wasn't taking careless risks with his relationship with this woman by jumping to conclusions again. He'd wait and see what she had to say at the meeting she'd requested and take it from there. First, she needed to learn she could trust him. Then he'd work on earning her confidences. Then...

But he was getting ahead of himself.

No longer interested in partying, he went looking for his hosts to make his farewells.

5

It was hard to settle to any of the multitude of tasks requiring his attention. Ben found himself worrying about Geni and her troubles. Wondering if he'd be able to make good on his promise to himself to protect her, and her son, from whoever was making her so afraid. And his gut instinct told him there *was* a 'someone', because fear was certainly what he'd detected in her unnatural reactions the night before.

He speculated uselessly on who it was she needed to talk to before she could tell *him* her story. He felt snubbed she was merely including him in what looked to be a professional courtesy to the women who cared for her son at school. How much more satisfying it would have been if she'd brought her story to him, as a woman looking to her man for support and protection.

Jealousy soured his mood because she wasn't going to be telling him exclusively. He wasn't important enough to her, he acknowledged reluctantly. And that intuitive gut of his twisted itself into knots as he realised how important *she* had become to *him*.

Impatient with pointless speculation, he reached for the phone to set up the appointment she'd asked for. That much he could do.

It scared him a little to realise just how much he wanted to be Geni Sullivan's man. Had been wanting it even when he believed her out of his reach; even though in thinking of her this way he was jumping the gun.

Until he had all the facts, there wasn't much he could do for her except to follow her lead.

He made the appointment with Jamie's teacher, Mrs Johnson, and Ms Marsden, then felt insulted all over again when he discovered Geni hadn't bothered to give him her personal number. He had to contact her via her office. Muttering impatiently to himself, he looked up the number and dialled, asking to be put through to Geni when Megan answered.

"Sorry Ben," Megan replied, "Geni's out this morning. She had some personal business to attend to. I'll get her to call you back, shall I?"

~~~~~

… so, you see why I'm feeling so scared, Sergeant Matthews," Geni concluded.

"Leave it with me, Lass. I'll get onto my contacts with the Victorians and see what I can find out. From what you've told me, though, we've still got a couple of weeks before we need go on full alert. Stay vigilant, and let me know if there's any new developments, and I'll get back to you as soon as I've got something to report. And Geni, try not to worry too much. You need to conserve your strength for when it might be needed."

"I'll try, Sergeant, but my instincts tell me the threat is very real. It's a horrible feeling, waiting for something bad to happen, while hoping against hope it won't, yet knowing in my heart that it's coming." Her words sounded garbled, even to herself, but Sergeant Matthews nodded, understanding exactly what she meant.

Geni reached across the desk to shake Don Matthew's hand, then marched briskly out of the police station and down the street, back to her office.

Just the far from easy act of sharing her worst fears with someone with the authority to provide real, practical assistance had somehow lightened her burden. Especially since the Sydney police had claimed to be unable to help her. Which, she grudgingly acknowledged was probably the truth at the time. Yet another reason her move to Oxley Crossing had been such a good idea.

Head raised, she smiled bravely as she took in the attractive streetscape with its iron-lace balconies, stained glass shop windows, and abundant street plantings of shrubs and flowers in tubs and hanging baskets.

Meeting Eddie Patterson heading in the opposite direction, she slowed to exchange greetings, adding another item to her mental list of Oxley Crossing's assets. People in this town looked out for their neighbours. More and more, she found herself identifying with this pretty country town, feeling she'd finally come home after years in the wilderness of inner-city Sydney.

On impulse she detoured into the Tan's bakery for a treat to share with Megan. At the same time, she invited Elizabeth and her husband, Geoff, to dinner on Friday evening.

It felt good, knowing she had friends, and, much as she was reluctant to, the time had come to let them in on her secrets. Her interview with Sergeant Don Matthews had convinced her of the inadvisability of trying to go it alone any longer.

~~~~~

"Ben Wright called. He wants you to call him back," Megan informed her, eyebrow raised in a silent question. Unable to wait, she followed it up with the question burning to be asked.

"Is there something going on between the two of you that you should be sharing with your best friend?"

"Nothing to tell. Yet. Maybe one day," Geni prevaricated, handing over the paper packet in her hand. Megan would accept the gentle rebuff. For now. But the pastries would soften her failure to confide in her friend.

"Ooh, Geoff Tan's cherry Danish. You shouldn't have Geni, but I'm glad you did." Although Megan accepted the abrupt change of subject, her look spoke volumes, letting Geni know it wasn't being forgotten. She could wait. Sooner or later Geni would be ready to talk to her.

"Why don't you call Ben while I put the kettle on?"

~~~~~

"Oh, thank you, Ben. That's perfect," Geni said, agreeing to the early meeting Ben had set up before school on Wednesday. "Now I won't have to take time off again for my personal stuff. And Ben," she added, "I'm sorry if I sounded a bit short with you last night. You took me by surprise and I didn't know what to say."

She mightn't have known what to say then, she thought, but she did now.

"Are you free for dinner on Friday? I'm asking a few friends round, and I'd really like it if you could come." She held her breath, waiting for his answer, wondering why inviting him into her home left her feeling shy and uncertain, when she had never been either before.

When Ben accepted almost before she'd finished speaking, a warm glow suffused her cheeks, leading her to impulsively blurt out, "Come early, Ben. Then we can talk before the others arrive."

While she had her phone in her hand, she also extended invitations to Eddie and Mike Patterson and Angie and Alan Morgan.

Between mouthfuls of cherry Danish, she gave Megan the bare bones, promising the full story later, and added her and Jon to her guest list.

It felt like marshalling her troops to guard her back. It felt good. Empowering. She only wished she'd found the courage to share her concern earlier, instead of struggling alone for so long.

~~~~~

That same evening, Geni waited till they had both finished eating before she sat Jamie down, knowing telling him would be a far more difficult task than telling anyone else.

This was Jamie's personal history. The truth about his own father. She drew in a deep breath, prayed for strength and courage, and got on with it.

"You haven't asked about your father very often, Jamie love," she began, "and when you have, I'm afraid I've lied to you because I felt you were too young for the truth. I wanted you to enjoy being a normal little boy, not one burdened by the knowledge of an awful family secret. I don't know whether I did the right thing or not."

When her son threw his arms around her in an impulsive hug, something he didn't often do now he was older, she breathed a huge sigh of relief and hugged him to her.

"It's okay Mum," her amazing son reassured her. "I didn't know you'd been lying to me. Not exactly, but I knew you didn't want to talk about my father, so I stopped asking. Do you remember my friend, Terry, from Sydney? Well, his parents were divorced too, but his mum made a photo album about his dad, and he came on visits, and sometimes he sent cards and presents and things."

Jamie glanced up at his mother's face, worried he might be upsetting her. Seeing she was smiling proudly at him, he continued.

"When I realised it wasn't like that with my father, I felt horrible for a while because I knew he must have been a bad man, or you would have been like Terry's mum."

He studied his mother's reaction to his words, then, swallowing a muffled sob, he sucked in a gusty breath.

"Are you going to tell me the truth now?"

He sounded wary and defensive. Fearful. As if he wasn't sure he was ready to hear the truth, whatever it was, and wished he was still too little to know.

Tears sprang into Geni's eyes, even though his pragmatic approach to the subject amazed her and filled her heart with pride. However, resolute in her purpose, she wiped the tears away.

Ignorance no longer had the power to protect Jamie from harm.

"Yes, Love. Things are happening which make it dangerous for me to put it off any longer. For your own safety, you need to know everything now."

He did need to know, but he was still only nine years old. Geni kept it simple and glossed over the worst of her story as briefly as possible. Even so, Jamie was sniffing back tears by the time she finished.

"My father is a really bad man, isn't he Mum? Does that mean I'm bad too, and will do bad things when I grow up?"

"Never. It doesn't work that way, Jamie. Badness isn't inherited like blond hair and green eyes." She smiled, ruffling his hair, feeling grateful he had inherited her colouring and finer bone structure, not Nigel's darker, heavier looks. "Being good or bad is something people choose for themselves. You already know the difference between right and wrong, and as long as you choose to do what's right, you'll never be bad. It's always going to be your choice, Jamie. You're the one in charge of your actions. Apart from me, there are lots of other people you can trust to advise you if you're not sure, you know." She kissed the top of his head and gave him another reassuring hug. When he swiped his arm across his face, smearing the tears that trickled down his cheeks, and wriggled free of her arms, she released him.

"I hope he never comes here," he uttered in a whispered shout. "I don't ever want to see him. Not even for visits. I won't have to, will I Mum?" Defiance crumbled to trembling uncertainty.

Her little boy's sadness and fear was almost more than Geni could bear. Especially as she couldn't make the promise he asked for with any degree of certainty. If Nigel took his paternity claim to court, he might very well be awarded visiting rights at the very least. Although that course of action sounded almost reassuringly normal.

What she truly feared was Nigel taking matters into his own hands; in which case anything at all could happen, with tragedy the possible outcome.

She hugged Jamie again, kissing his sweet, upturned face.

"I'm doing all I can to keep you safe, Darling Boy. You can help by being careful. I'll tell you when it becomes specially important."

~~~~~

The dining table needed to be fully extended to accommodate all of Geni's new friends. Ben, responding to her invitation to arrive early, was there in time to help her rearrange the furniture.

"I can understand you don't want everyone in town gossiping about your situation," he commented, "but why did you wait so long before telling us at the school about Jamie possibly being in danger if there's a custody battle with his father? We can't protect him if we don't know the situation."

Geni put down the handful of cutlery with which she was laying the table, and straightened to her full, less-than-impressive, height. She had known Ben would have questions, and if she wanted the opportunity to build something good from their strong mutual attraction, then she would have to give him the answers he asked for. All of them. Without honesty, there would be no building of trust between them, and therefore no future to look forward to.

If she had a future. Her stomach quivered as dread flooded her being.

Unfortunately, Ben was the type of honourable man who would try to take her burdens upon his own broad shoulders. Which was not entirely what she wanted.

To be the strong woman she aspired to being, she had to learn to stand up for herself. She would be treading a fine line between accepting Ben's help, while protecting *him* as best she could from danger, since all her previous reasons for not getting involved, with anyone, still applied. Only more so, because of how she felt about him.

"I was too scared of word getting back to whoever Nigel had set to watch us, and deliver his notes, to tell anyone. Not even Megan. Until you told me you wanted more than just simple friendship with me, I hadn't found the courage to speak out. I've discovered during this week how sharing my fears makes me stronger. Better able to face up to them, as I'm able to draw strength from others. From my friends. Now I wish I *had* done so sooner."

She walked round the table to stand close to him, gazing earnestly into his face.

Ben couldn't resist the temptation and leaned down to brush a soft kiss across her lips, but he had more questions. Too many to allow himself to be side-tracked, no matter how much he'd prefer to make love with Geni. His pulse quickened when she didn't reject him outright, but he wanted to fully understand the situation, and they didn't have much time before the other dinner guests arrived. Regretfully, he dropped his hands from her shoulders and stepped back, breaking contact. Returning to the subject.

"You mentioned on Wednesday that your ex-husband has been making threats against you," he said, leading her to the sofa and sitting down at her side, slewed around to face her while they talked. "What kind of threats did you mean, Geni? You weren't very specific the other morning."

"Let me show you. Sergeant Matthews heard back from his contacts in the Victorian Police that Nigel's cellmate was released a short time before I started getting these notes hand-delivered into my mailbox. This bloke, Kevin Simpson, has been traced to an address just a few blocks from where Jamie and I lived. Sergeant Matthews suspects he's been doing Nigel's dirty work for him."

She jumped up and hurried into her bedroom, returning in moments with the bundle of notes and photos, thrusting them into Ben's hands.

He read through them, looking sharply at her once or twice, then flicked through them a second time, this time reading between the lines of what at first glance appeared quite innocuous expressions of hope for their shared future as a family when Nigel returned home to her and his son. As if he was merely away on a trip, or for work.

Innocuous, until one recalled they had been divorced for over eight years, and that both the divorce, and Nigel's prison sentence, were due to his physical abuse of Geni during their short marriage. Then they did appear weird and threatening. The photos, demonstrating the sender of the notes knew exactly where Geni lived and worked, and where Jamie went to school, were particularly disturbing. Ben's lips compressed into a white, angry line, and his eyes blazed.

"Bloody Hell, Geni. Why didn't you go to the police with these as soon as you started getting them?"

"But I did. And I kept going, every time a new one arrived. Only with Nigel still locked up in a different state, they said their hands were tied. None of those letters contains an overt threat, you see. It's only because I know what he's like that I interpreted them as such. There's no way I'll ever go back to him. I'll do whatever I have to, to keep Jamie out of his hands as well." She shuddered, lips trembling.

"I can't even take out a restraining order against him at this stage. I have to wait until he actually does something actionable. By then it might be too late." Geni took a moment to dab at the tears forming in her eyes.

"When the photo of Jamie outside his school arrived, I went into panic mode. Megan had just invited me to join her here in Oxley Crossing, so I resigned, telling everyone I was moving to Queensland. I left Sydney very quietly, without telling anyone where I was really going. There has been nothing since. No letters or photos, but Nigel doesn't get out for another couple of weeks, so, although I appear to have made a clean getaway, I'm not relaxing my guard yet." She took a moment to catch her breath.

"I can't take the risk," she continued. "Sergeant Matthews has been wonderfully supportive, finding out as much as he can, and asking his contacts to keep a watch on Nigel and his cellmate, Kevin Simpson. I told Jamie what's happening, and I warned you and his teachers at the school. Tonight, I'm telling the rest of my friends. I want as many people watching out for Jamie as possible."

"You matter too, Geni." Ben swallowed the lump in his throat. He'd never fancied himself as a knight in shining armour, and shied away from such a romantic image, but he did feel a fierce need to protect Geni and her son. His woman. His *family*. And what a time this was to realise the depth of his feelings for Geni, when her worries made it a selfish imposition to speak them aloud. He resolved to let his actions speak for him, but he felt so helplessly inadequate.

"Don't put yourself at risk, Geni. You need to be careful of your own safety as well as Jamie's. You'll be no use to him if anything happens to you. Will you trust me to be here for you? I'll drop everything and come whenever you call."

"Oh, Ben. I do trust you. But you can see, can't you, that I can't afford to be seen with another man if Nigel does turn up, wanting me back. He'd be likely to attack anyone he perceived as standing in his way." The pleading eyes she turned on him were enough to melt the hardest of hearts, but Ben resisted. Her concern for *his* safety was almost an insult.

"Give me some credit, Geni. I might not go around getting into bar-room brawls, but I keep fit, and I can handle myself when it matters. I don't need to hide behind your skirts." Ben bristled at the perceived slur upon his masculinity, until Geni interrupted him.

"I'm sure you can fight if you have to, Ben. I have no doubts on that score. The problem is, Ben, if Nigel does come after me, and sees I have a man paying attention to me, it'll send him into a rage. Then it will be worse for me if he gets me on my own. I'd rather have you as my secret weapon. Please, Ben. Do it my way?"

At the arrival of several other guests just then, Geni squeezed his hand and hurried off to answer the door, not waiting for his reply, and Ben used the time to think over the implications of what she had said.

He understood her reasoning, but it didn't sit well with him to leave a woman, *his* woman, to face danger on her own. He decided to bide his time until he could once again speak to Geni alone. By which time he might have a better idea on how to proceed.

Geni also bided her time, waiting till all her guests were sitting comfortably with tea and coffee after dinner, the kitchen clean-up all finished, before introducing the subject predominantly occupying her mind.

"I'm glad you were all able to join me tonight, and a special thank you to you, Elizabeth, for arranging for Jamie to have a sleep-over with Bailey at your parents' house, as I have an ulterior motive, beyond the pleasure of your company, for my invitation tonight."

She took a moment to compose her thoughts. First, looking anxiously towards Megan, she apologised.

"I should have told you all this as soon as it started, Megan. At the very latest, before accepting your partnership offer. I hope you can forgive me..."

"Oh, Geni," Megan broke in. "I'll always forgive you. We're best friends, aren't we?"

"You haven't heard all of what's going on, yet."

"Doesn't matter. I'm just glad you're finally coming clean."

"Okay. Well. You know, I count all of you, everyone here in this room, as my friends. When I decided I had to tell you all, it seemed easier for me to tell you together. Rather than repeating myself over and over."

"That sounds reasonable, Dear," Eddie voiced her support. "You go ahead."

When Geni finished telling her friends how she was being stalked by her abusive ex-husband, shortly to be released from prison, a spate of conversation erupted, aimed mostly at ways they could best help and protect her. And Jamie. None of them forgot the innocent child caught in the middle. Geni's heart filled to bursting with how lucky, and how proud she was, to be accepted without reservations by this stalwart group. Not even her now-cold coffee wiped the tremulous smile from her face.

"We've got your back." Megan, one hand resting protectively on her pregnant belly, leaned forward from the shelter of her husband's arms to pull Geni into an awkward one-armed hug.

"Right Jon?"

"For sure. We live closest to you, and we'll hear if you yell. Day or night, Geni. Don't hesitate. I'll rig up an alarm system and keep my eyes open when Jamie's playing in the backyard."

"Speaking of Jamie," Mike offered, "you tell him he can come to us anytime, if he needs a safe refuge."

"Us too," chipped in Geoff, with a quick glance at Elizabeth, who nodded her confirmation of his offer. "Mum and Dad aren't here, but I'm sure they'll be only too happy to be another safe house for him."

"If he's in danger at home, he can sleep over with Bailey and we'll keep him hidden," Elizabeth added.

By the time Angie chimed in affirming Geni's decision to stand up for herself, and Alan volunteered 'Morgan's Run' as yet another safe haven, for both her son and herself, tears were streaming down Geni's face. It was such a huge relief, knowing she was no longer alone.

Shortly after that, the gathering began to break up, and Geni soon found herself alone with Ben once again. First to arrive, he was now making sure he was the last to leave. She put the kettle on again as he looked to have something on his mind. When she went to sit in an armchair, he reached out to steer her to the sofa, settling himself at her side. He put down his coffee mug to take her hand in both of his comfortingly large ones.

"Everything the others said goes for me too, you know."

"I know." Geni squeezed his hand.

"But I think there's more to the story than you told us. I don't know a lot about these matters, but your ex seems to have been given an unusually long sentence for a case of domestic violence. Not that he doesn't deserve it, mind you."

It wasn't quite a question, but Geni treated it as one.

"You're right, Ben. There is more."

She took a deep breath, letting it out slowly to steady her nerves.

"As I said earlier, I was young and stupid when I married Nigel. He was a big, take-charge guy, and I mistakenly read his extreme possessiveness as him being protective. It wasn't until later I realised how effectively he'd cut me off from all my friends, and especially from my Gran who brought me up. He'd moved us to Melbourne where I had no job and no friends. When he started getting physical, I had no-one to turn to for help. He was always very sweet afterwards, promising not to hurt me again, but his violence escalated, until I ran away, afraid he'd harm the baby I was carrying. Gran took me in, but when he discovered I'd left him, he followed me, bursting into the house, demanding I go back with him." Her voice shook, and tears began flowing silently.

Ben pressed a clean handkerchief into her hands, helping her mop her wet cheeks.

"Sorry Ben. I can't seem to stop crying tonight. I'm not usually such a weak sister."

"I'm the one who should be apologising. I didn't mean to upset you. You don't have to tell me anything if you don't want to."

"No. No, I'm alright now. I think it will do me good to unburden myself, if you can bear to hear it all."

By now, Ben had wrapped his warm, sheltering arms around her. Snuggling her close against his side, he dropped a kiss onto the top of her head. If she could bear to tell it, then he could bear to listen.

"You see, another mistake I made in the beginning was thinking how lovely it was that Nigel was a devout Christian." Geni paused to wipe away fresh tears.

"By the time I learned he used the Bible as a mask to disguise his true character, it was too late. He would quote scripture at me, then 'chastise' me for imaginary transgressions. There was nothing Christian about his behaviour behind closed doors."

A shudder rocked her body, and Ben cradled her even closer in his arms.

"The longer I stayed with him, the more dangerous, and, I believe unstable, he sounded when he ranted on at me, trying to justify the beatings he gave me. At the end, at my Gran's, when I refused to go back to him, he hit me, knocking me down and dragging me out to his car. I fought him every inch, hoping help would arrive in time. Gran called the police, and we could hear the sirens getting closer."

She took a moment to simply breath, then continued her story.

"That's when he got desperate, and deliberately broke my arm, to stop me fighting him so he could force me into his car. Gran was hitting him with her umbrella, trying to slow him down. He swung round, punching her hard. She fell down and hit her head on the brick edging of a garden bed. He killed her Ben! He killed Gran! And it was all my fault!"

Overcome by emotion, she buried her face in Ben's chest, sobbing in earnest.

Ben held her close, rubbing her back and making soothing murmurs against her hair.

"Not your fault, Geni," he repeated over and over. "He was the one in the wrong."

As her bout of weeping tailed off into wet sniffles, Geni slipped her arms around his torso, raising her tear-drenched face to him.

"If I'd listened to Gran, I'd never have got involved with him, so some of the blame is mine, Ben. Anyway..." Hardly daring to meet his eyes, she concluded her own personal horror story.

"The police charged him with a whole list of offences, from manslaughter to causing actual bodily harm and resisting arrest. I filed for divorce immediately, but he refused to accept reality, ranting in court that I was still his wife, joined to him by God. Saying no divorce would change that. He said I'd better be waiting for him when he got out. He said he'd be back for me and his son. You've seen those notes. He's saying exactly the same things in them. I believe his attitude hasn't changed. I'm scared, Ben. He'll be released in a few days now. What if he finds out where I am?"

"You're not alone this time, Geni Darling. You've got me, and a whole host of good friends, including Don Matthews and the whole New South Wales Police Force backing him-up. If Nigel tries it on again, Don can be relied on to use the full force of the law. Besides, maybe the letters were all bluff, to give you a nasty fright, and he won't bother chasing after you after all this time. Oxley Crossing is a long way from Melbourne."

"Well, he succeeded, if that was his aim. They did give me a nasty fright. I'm still frightened," she muttered, the words muffled against his chest.

Ben slipped a finger under her chin, tilting her face to meet his lips in a gentle kiss. A kiss that seemed to go on blissfully forever, soothing her jangled nerves.

Geni forgot her fears, lost in the heady wonder of their first kiss. Her lips parted of their own volition, deepening the kiss. Ben's tongue stroked the inside of her mouth rousing her to a passionate response.

Coming up for air, Ben whispered, hoarsely, "Shall I stay with you tonight, Darling?"

Geni was tempted. Her mouth shaping a 'Yes', at the last moment she shook her head. She didn't understand why, but Ben – the way she felt about him – was different to any boyfriends she'd had in the past. Ben was special.

If she made love with Ben, she would be committing her whole future into his hands. Hers and Jamie's. She wasn't ready. Even though she suspected she was falling in love with him, she wasn't ready. Even though she felt certain she could trust him.

She recalled all her excellent reasons for keeping him at a distance until this issue with Nigel was resolved.

If she ever placed herself in a man's hands again, it would be as a strong, equal partner, not as a needy supplicant. If that man should prove to be Ben Wright, she wanted him to be proud to have her by his side, not pitying her for being a frail, clinging vine. There was only one answer she could give to his question, much as she wished it could be otherwise.

"Not tonight, Ben. It wouldn't be right."

Determined to be as unlike Nigel as he could be, Ben accepted her refusal with good grace. It wasn't as if he'd really thought she would agree, simply that he'd got carried away in the heat of the moment. He wanted her, but he didn't think he was really ready for her.

When he made love to Geni Sullivan, and he hoped it would be soon, he didn't want any shadows between them. He wanted her to commit herself fully to sharing her life with him, and, he suspected, she was a long way from making such a commitment. He was planning long-term. Just as well, as it looked as if he might have to wait quite a while.

One last passionate kiss to sustain him, and he bade her farewell.

"I'll wait outside till I hear you lock the door, Darling. Goodnight."

6

It felt peculiar, waking up to silence, knowing she was alone in the flat. It happened so rarely she couldn't remember the last time. Genie lay in bed savouring the peace. The quiet. And, the memory of being kissed by Ben Wright the evening before. At the time, she had been too off balance to properly appreciate how sweet and encouraging it felt being held against his broad, firm chest. How knee-meltingly exciting it had felt being kissed by those firm, sensuous, lips.

If she was lucky, he'd be looking for a repeat performance. Soon.

And if he did, she'd make sure she was ready to reciprocate.

Not dating while danger threatened didn't have to exclude getting to know each other better, and what nicer way was there to get to know a man than through delicious, shared kisses? When the man in question roused her to nerve-tingling awareness simply by meeting her eyes across the room and smiling his warm, slow smile, well… The possibilities were breathtaking.

How she wished Nigel Blount's dark, shadowy presence wasn't looming over her, poisoning what would otherwise be such an enjoyable phase of her life – a wonderful new job where she was her own boss, a new home, new friends added to old and a potentially promising new relationship. All of which had to be put on hold because she'd made one huge, stupid mistake when she was young and naïve.

Remembering cast a shadow over her happy mood. Uttering a very rude expletive, she headed for the shower. Jamie would be home soon, bringing Bailey with him. Their cricket team was playing their last home game on the sports field across the street, and she needed to pack up some drinks and snacks and see that Jamie had left his cricket gear ready.

Arriving at the game an hour later with the two boys strutting proudly ahead of her in cricket whites already showing signs of recent hard usage, the first person she laid eyes on was Ben. Naturally, since his was the figure she instinctively searched for. A revealing blush infusing her cheeks with colour, she looked shyly away, pretending to scrabble for something in the depths of the capacious bag dangling from her arm. When she allowed herself to look up again, it was to see he had changed direction, making a beeline for her, the corners of his lips turning upward in a quirky, welcoming grin guaranteed to set her pulse racing.

"Geni. Boys. Good morning. Jamie, would you and Bailey take your mother's chair and set it up over there next to Melanie Morgan's mum. I've got a favour to ask you, Geni. Alan and I have to play in the All-Age team on the main oval," he gestured towards the nearby historic grandstand where a crowd was gathering.

"Alan's father, Andrew Morgan, is relieving me as coach, and I was hoping you might help Angie as acting manager?"

"Sure, Ben. I'd be happy to." Feeling unreasonably let down, Geni turned to follow the boys.

"Geni." Ben reached out, and although barely touching her arm with his fingertips, it was enough to bring her to a halt, eagerly turning back to face him.

"It's good to see you. You know, last night's kiss whetted my appetite for more." His voice had lowered to a barely audible whisper, his smile growing intimately inviting. Geni felt her cheeks heating again. "When the kids finish up, will you come over and watch my game? I'll carry your stuff home afterwards," he coaxed. Not that she needed further persuasion.

"I'd like that, Ben, but it's going to depend on what the boys want to do."

There was no time for more. Jon, also in cricket whites, jogged up to them

"Come on Ben. We lost the toss and you're needed on the field."

As it happened, Angie was also staying on till the men finished playing, and the boys happily joined the pack of children in the playground alongside the oval, drifting back periodically for drinks and snacks.

The Oxley Crossing team was batting by the time Geni and Angie found seats in the home team section of the stands. Alan, one of the openers, was already out, and came to join them, sprawling alongside his wife, laughing with her at his lack of success.

Jon, padded up ready to take the field, sat in front of them beside Megan who was the team's official scorekeeper, and, when Geni looked for him, she spied Ben taking his place at the wicket where he replaced Joey lambert who had just been caught out for a duck.

It was pure pleasure for Geni to sit back and feast her eyes on Ben's trim, athletic masculinity without arousing speculation in the minds of perspicacious observers such as Eddie Patterson who was sitting close by. She groaned with everyone else when he almost got run out by his partner and cheered with parochial enthusiasm when he hit a boundary. Another gasp as the man at first slip dropped a sitter, then Ben and his partner settled into a comfortable rhythm, the score creeping up steadily towards the target. Until disaster struck, and Ben was bowled out for a respectable thirty-eight runs. Geni, along with the rest of the home team supporters, clapped him off the field as Jon picked up his bat and ran out to take his chances facing the opposition's star bowler.

Ben waved a genial hand, acknowledging everyone in their section of the stands, but his flashing smile was directed towards Geni alone. He dropped his bat into his open kit-bag and stripped off his pads, tossing them in on top. In her mind, Geni imagined him stripping off even more. Imagined the ripple of toned muscles beneath bare suntanned skin, then abruptly pulled her thoughts into line. The middle of a crowded cricket match was hardly the place to indulge herself in erotic daydreams. Her lips twitched into an embarrassed smile and she almost giggled aloud at her foolishness. Until the shadow haunting her life reminded her that this was certainly not the time for such dreams, either.

Still, she couldn't deny the thrill of sharpened anticipation when Ben scooped up his water bottle and climbed the stands to the vacant space to her left. A narrow space, which necessitated close bodily contact from knee to shoulder as she shuffled up to let him squeeze into it.

"A good innings," she congratulated him, struck by sudden shyness which wiped her mind of any more profound observation. Fortunately, there were plenty of others under no such constraint, so she leaned back in her seat and let the conversation flow over her. A pervasive warmth infused her, generated from the multiple points of contact between herself and the man pressed up against her side. Without thinking, she leaned in, ever so slightly, deepening the pressure. As an answering movement of strong, hard muscle and bone discreetly caressed her in return, her eyes flicked up to discover him watching her, expressive gray eyes informing her she wasn't alone in enjoying the secret pleasure. Geni had never in her life experienced such subtle love-making, the public arena providing additional titillation.

By the time the match concluded an hour later, with a resounding win to the visitors, Geni's nerves fizzed and sparked from the prolonged siege upon her defences, sweet though it had been. Unsure of what action she should take, she was relieved to see Elizabeth strolling up to thank her for minding Bailey for the afternoon; which allowed her to defer the decision and step away from Ben's possessive hand helping her up from the bench.

"He could have gone to his grandmother as usual, Geni," Elizabeth said, "but I'm sure it was much more fun for him to spend the afternoon with his friends."

Just then the boys came running up, their maltreated whites now so far from pristine, Geni wondered if they could possibly be restored. In future, she mentally noted, she'd once again need to get into the habit of carrying a change of clothes for Jamie as she had when he was an infant.

"Oh good," Jamie exclaimed, all wide-eyed innocence. "You and Mrs Tan are both here, Mum. Bailey and I," he glanced sideways, seeking corroborative support from his co-conspirator, "were just thinking."

Here it comes, Geni thought, working to repress an amused grin. She was rapidly growing accustomed to the dynamics of this pair, her heart lifting to see her son behaving so naturally. So happily. Jamie, accurately interpreting her pseudo-stern expression, grinned and blithely continued.

"You know, Mum, Mrs Tan has to work tomorrow as well. Me and Bailey wondered if you'd like to go for another picnic at Rainbow Falls? Last time was really good fun."

"Bailey and I," Geni automatically corrected his grammar while engaging in an unspoken conversation with Elizabeth.

In case any further persuasion was needed, Jamie added, "Mel and Jocelyn are asking their parents too, Mum, so you'd have friends to talk to as well."

Sure enough, when Geni cast an eye over her shoulder, she saw another parent/child conference taking place a few metres away.

Angie caught her eye and raised a brow. Geni looked to Elizabeth, who nodded, then she gave Angie a thumbs-up, and the matter was decided.

This would be the last week for an indefinite period when she could allow Jamie the sweet freedom of being a normal little boy, and she was determined not to curtail his activities until she absolutely had to. Quickly, she put the shadow of dark thoughts behind her, giving her full attention to her son.

The details quickly settled with Elizabeth, Geni reached to pick up her bag, and bumped into a solid body standing very close at her back. Ben. She hadn't exactly forgotten him, but for a short time Jamie had superseded him in her consciousness. She half-turned towards him, an uncertain smile on her lips, as he bent to whisper in her ear.

"The picnic sounds fun. If you were serious about not dating, Geni, I'll respect your wishes, but you did say you'd be happy to spend time with me if we were both in the same place at the same time. I reckon you can count on my feeling the urge to go swimming at the Falls tomorrow."

On the spur of the moment, Geni decided that what was good for Jamie could be applied equally to herself. For the next week she would simply enjoy life as it came.

"I'll be looking forward to it, Ben." She gave a soft chuckle. "Shall I pack food for you, too?"

"Only if you let me bring the drinks."

"And I'll send some hamburger rolls and pastries with Bailey," Elizabeth chimed in, showing there was nothing wrong with her hearing.

The conspiratorial wink accompanying her words assured them both that this was one piece of gossip she would keep to herself.

Her intellect every bit as sharp as her hearing, she had already intuited that for some as yet unknown reason, they were keeping their burgeoning feelings for each other under wraps.

"Right then. I promised to carry your gear home, Geni. Let's go. Bye everyone." There was a tinge of colour in his lean, tanned cheeks as he nodded to Elizabeth; colour attributable to neither the sun, nor bending down to pick up Geni's bag and fold-up chair.

On ushering Jamie and Ben through her door, Geni sent her son off to shower and change.

"I want to soak those disgusting whites immediately, or I'll never get all the dirt and grass stains out," she told him, forestalling his incipient protest at having to bath so early, "so take them straight to the laundry for me."

Jamie was barely out of sight when Ben reached for her, his lips descending to claim hers in a fierce, heady kiss.

"God, Geni. Sitting next to you all afternoon and having to keep my hands to myself, was torture."

"I know. Same here," she murmured in reply. "But such sweet torture, don't you think?"

She clasped her hands round his neck and rose on tip-toes meeting him more than half-way. They remained where they'd stalled on entering the flat, lost in each other until Jamie's voice caused them to reluctantly draw apart.

"Dirty clothes in the laundry, Mum," he shouted, almost simultaneously with the bathroom door being slammed shut.

Seconds later the sound of the shower running could be heard.

"Do you think he saw?" *Damn!* Ben thought. He'd not given a moment's thought to how the boy might react to seeing him kissing his mother. How irresponsible could he be?

"Probably not." Geni's unconcerned tone relieved his conscience as much as her prosaic words. "There's no clear sight-line from here, but I'll talk to him if he says anything."

Relief gave way to another emotion entirely, as Ben cynically thought that maybe Jamie had seen his mother in a man's arms often enough to take it for granted. Jealousy colouring his thoughts, he coolly took another step back, putting a safe distance between them.

"I'd better be going," he said. *Before I say something I might regret*, he added silently. His rational mind told him he had no right to be jealous, but he'd shocked himself more than once by the intensity of the emotions this woman aroused in him. Guiltily, he reminded himself that Geni had troubles enough without him adding to them. He bent to retrieve his bag of cricket gear.

"Don't go." A dizzying mix of desire and happiness made Geni reckless.

"Stay for dinner. That's if you'd like to?" she added, suddenly unsure, her voice turning the words into a question. Maybe he was glad of an excuse to leave.

"Oh, I like, alright."

He kissed her again, releasing her immediately when, smiling happily once more, she pushed gently against his chest.

"I'd better start the dinner. Jamie will be back in a few minutes, absolutely ravenous and claiming to be dying of hunger, in spite of everything he ate during the afternoon."

"Let me help."

Geni stared at Ben for a long moment. He wasn't the first man to attract her interest since the traumatic ending of her short-lived marriage, but he was the first she'd invited into her own space. Jamie's home. All others, not that there'd been so very many, she had met with on neutral ground.

None of those others, she realised with a rush of melting warmth, had been as considerate of her needs, her wishes, as this man. And now he was offering to help in the kitchen. In her mind she heard a chorus of female voices advising her that in Ben Wright she had hit the jackpot. An assessment with which she concurred whole-heartedly.

Now all she had to do was navigate past the dangers threatening her son and herself, and hope he was still standing tall at her side if...

No. Not if. When.

She'd pray long and earnestly that he was there for them both *when* they won through to safety. With a little shake of her head, she pulled herself out of her moment of introspection to smile broadly at the man whose face still bore a smear of rose-pink lipstick from their kisses. A dead giveaway. She grabbed a tissue from the box on the counter and wiped it off.

"How are you with salads?" she asked, turning to toss the soiled tissue into the kitchen tidy.

Ben blinked, dazzled by the blazing happiness of her smile.

Assured he considered himself a dab hand with a fresh garden salad, Geni set him up with ingredients and equipment, then busied herself making pasta and garlic bread. When Jamie, hungry as predicted, wandered into the kitchen, she assigned him the task of laying the table. Working companionably alongside Ben and her son, Geni felt a rare contentment. They fitted together with ease, almost as if they were, all three of them, a family. The feeling continued throughout the cheerfully relaxed meal and afterwards, when Ben insisted she sit down while he and Jamie took care of the dishes. This was followed by a riotous game of Monopoly, and when Jamie's bedtime rolled round, Geni wasn't at all surprised by his confiding whisper as she tucked him in.

"Mum, Mr Wright's really cool. I think he really likes you, don't you? I wish he was my father and not the bad man."

Carefully noncommittal, she suggested, "Why don't you add it to your prayers?"

Half an hour later, she was disgruntled to find herself alone in the lounge room. She knew she'd been the one to set the ground rules, but still...

It had been a considerable disappointment to have Ben kiss her to the point of total surrender, then abruptly take his leave.

~~~~~

The remainder of that week was more of the same. A circumspect and very proper Ben Wright was never far from Geni's side when she went out. Although very quick to point out to her friends they were *not* dating, she was, nevertheless, subjected to quite a few knowing looks.

From Angie at the Sunday picnic at Rainbow Falls, to Elizabeth after cricket training on Wednesday evening, to Eddie and Megan at the regular Friday night dinner at The Victoria Inn.

Following the Sunday church service, Geni found herself being quietly steered into a deserted corner of the churchyard by Sergeant Don Matthews. A move which had several of her friends staring after her with varying degrees of concern.

"I'll only keep you a moment, Geni," Don began. "I believe it's best all round if I keep you informed."

A sentiment with which Geni nodded her decided approval, although her heart sank at the reminder.

"Nigel Blount was released from Barwon Prison on Thursday, as per schedule. He caught a train into Melbourne, checked into the half-way house as instructed, then dropped off the radar the next day. The Victorian police haven't a clue where he is, and apparently couldn't care less since he's now a free man and hasn't committed a crime; but I want you to know our boys in Sydney are keeping a watchful eye on that dodgy mate of his – Kevin Simpson. We reckon there's a good chance Blount will show up if he's seriously planning to make a move against you and your boy. In the meantime, I've asked for the Highway Patrol to step-up their activities out this way."

He turned sympathetic eyes on her, wishing he had something more reassuring to report. An old-fashioned police officer, he had very strong personal ideas on how brutes like this Nigel Blount ought to be treated; and they didn't include letting them run free to terrorise defenceless women and children.

"Time to implement some of those precautions we discussed, Lass. No need to go overboard just yet, though."

He gave her arm a comforting pat.

"I'll keep you in the loop. Soon as I hear anything, I'll pass it on; and you keep me posted on any new developments at your end."

"Yes. Yes, I will. Thank you, Sergeant. You can't imagine how relieved I am to see you taking me seriously."

"Actually, my dear, I can imagine it. This is not the first case like yours to come to my attention. You be careful, now." He patted her hand then took himself off.

FINDING MR WRIGHT

7

"Geni, what's up? What did Don say to you?"

Megan grabbed Geni by the arm, anxiety adding urgency to her tone. Her friend had the pale, shaken look of a person who had just received bad news. Several others with whom Geni had shared her secret, gathered around her in a protective circle, Ben surreptitiously slipping a strong hand beneath her elbow.

Shaking off the appalling sense of helplessness which had momentarily rendered her pale and frozen to the spot, Geni rapidly took stock of the small crowd of morning worshippers gathered in front of the church. Locating Jamie, laughing and playing some complicated game of tag with the other children, she relaxed visibly and addressed her concerned supporters.

"Sergeant Matthews just told me…" Hearing how jerky and breathless her words sounded, Geni took a moment to steady herself. Encouraged by the light squeeze Ben gave her elbow, she began again, this time in full control of her voice, giving the gist of Don's words as succinctly as possible. It wasn't something she wanted to dwell on, or endlessly hash over with anyone, friends or not.

"Nigel's out, and he's disappeared. The police have no idea where he is, although they're watching for him. Don advised me to be careful."

"Just as well then, we had the security guys here on Friday to put in the new cameras covering your office and flat," Jon said, putting a protective arm around Megan.

Mindful of the fact that, apart from Jon, there were mainly women and older blokes like himself and his service station manager, Jack O'Hara, working in what had been designated the target area – Geni's flat, Megan's office suite and the bank which shared her building – Mike Patterson had ordered new CCTV cameras. Talking to the agent for the security company, he mentioned the reason for upgrading in a quiet little backwater like Oxley Crossing, and she obliged by expediting the work.

In the sure knowledge that if Nigel did come after Geni and his son, he would have to have his own transport, Don had not only approved the work, but had provided up-to-date photos of both Nigel Blount and his mate Kevin Simpson. Accompanying the photos had been a stern warning that nobody should take matters into their own hands.

Mike's response had been to ensure they all had a direct line to the local police station on speed dial.

In addition, all who had offered their homes as safe houses had checked their window and door locks. In a couple of instances, new ones had been fitted.

At first it worried Geni when she noticed Jamie appeared to be treating the whole situation as an exciting new game.

On the whole, though, she decided it was probably better than having him stricken with fear and terrified of his own shadow.

Jamie wasn't nearly as happy with the measures Ms Marsden insisted on at the school, starting this week, although Geni was more than happy to comply.

Carolyn Marsden insisted on pre-empting any possible danger of Jamie being unlawfully taken from the school grounds by his father, by ruling that in the morning, he be accompanied until handed over to the teacher on duty, and in the afternoons, wait in the office to be collected. During playtimes, he was again to report to the duty teacher and not wander off out of sight.

"If need be, Ms Sullivan," she concluded when informing Geni of her decisions, "we can remove him from the playground entirely, letting him spend lunchtime in the library, which some children actually consider a privilege."

She smiled as she said it, but Geni felt comforted, knowing she meant every word

When Ben added his support to Ms Marsden, speaking to Jamie himself, he was unsurprised when the boy sulked and held himself aloof, where previously, he had been subjected to a mild case of hero-worship. It hurt, but he was used to boys, and it didn't change a thing in his estimation.

He was there for the Sullivan's whether Jamie liked it or not. And young Jamie would be protected, whether he liked the stringent measures they were taking or not.

Now, after Don's warning that Nigel was on the loose and unaccounted for, Geni resolved to keep Jamie very close.

After school he could do his homework in the office kitchen and play in the securely fenced backyard until she finished work and was free to go with him to the park to join the other children. Another move which did not find favour with the gregarious nine-year-old.

"Please, Jamie Darling," she pleaded, when his face set in a mulish pout. "Please. Do it for me, so I don't have to worry about you. Just until this is all over."

Jamie squirmed, studiously avoiding her gaze, then reluctantly suggested an amendment to the scheme.

"Can Bailey stay with me?" A vigorous argument obviously trembled on his lips, and Geni wisely leapt to accept this small concession.

"Yes, he can, Darling. If he wants to and his mother agrees."

That was good enough for Jamie, who had no fears whatever about being abandoned by his best friend.

"Okay, then," he agreed, wriggling to be set free when his relieved mother clasped him to her in an enthusiastic bear hug.

8

At bloody last!

Nigel 'Butch' Blount savoured the taste of freedom as the gates of HM Prison Barwon clanged shut behind him. His sentence had dragged interminably. Unchanging boredom as day followed identical day with never so much as a visitor to break the monotony of his regimented existence.

Yet another issue he'd be taking up with Eugenie when he caught up with her. Other blokes who'd been sent down for far worse than him had received regular visits from wives and families, but not his wife. He hadn't seen hide nor hair of her since he'd been dragged out of the courtroom after that incompetent bloody judge had handed down his sentence.

She'd pay for abandoning him without a word, along with all the rest of the long list of her offences he'd compiled over the years. He'd worried she might have taken up with another man, thinking that stupid divorce she'd got gave her a licence to disregard her marriage vows, but Kev had assured him she was still on her own.

Except for the kid.

His son.

He scowled, thinking of how his son had been forced to grow up without his father to steer him in the right direction. From what he'd heard other inmates saying about their kids, he was afraid his boy might have developed a lot of unacceptable bad habits. It looked as if he was going to have his hands full when he caught up with the pair of them.

He brooded on his grievances all the way into Geelong where he could catch a train to Melbourne. Eugenie was going to pay dearly for her defiance. If not for her intransigence, he would never have been in that Godforsaken hellhole of Barwon Prison. Resentment boiled into a smouldering rage as he turned his gaze inward, reliving yet again the incident that had unjustly landed him in gaol.

In Butch's egocentric mind the facts had conveniently rearranged themselves. The courts had labelled him a wife-beater, but it said in the bible a man had both the right and the duty to chastise his wife. When she failed in *her* duty to her husband, it was only fitting that the chastisement be appropriate to her sins. Wilfully removing herself and his unborn son from his patriarchal care warranted the most severe of punishments.

Punishments which had yet to be administered, owing to the undue interference of that stupid old bag. How dared she call the police? He wasn't at all sorry she'd ended up dead, but it wasn't his fault.

No way. He wasn't some crazed killer.

As for the manslaughter charge, which the bloody prosecutor had tried to have upped to murder, that was all a damned fabrication. He hadn't touched the vicious old harpy. *She* had come at him, hitting and jabbing him with an umbrella, of all the ridiculous things. He'd been in danger of losing an eye when he fended her off and she tripped over her own feet and fell.

His facile mind easily omitted the full-force punch to the side of the old lady's face which had been the true cause of her fall. A punch witnessed by a number of goggling bystanders as well as the police who'd just arrived on the scene at that moment. Butch blamed his lawyer for failing to convince the jury of his innocence.

And, most of all, his traitorous wife!

His lawyer was beyond his reach, but she wasn't. Not for much longer.

At the trial he'd tried to explain matters himself, interjecting with his version of the truth in court, but that biased idiot sitting on the bench as if he was God almighty, had ordered him dragged from the courtroom. How was that fair? Refusing to let him be heard. Butch glared impotently at the back of the hapless bus driver's head, silently reiterating his vow that never again would he allow himself to be subjected to such a humiliating debacle.

He'd kill anyone who tried it.

In Melbourne later that day, he checked into the half-way house as instructed, mainly because he had no money to go anywhere else. He'd been enrolled in a program aimed at integrating him back into society. As if he needed such rubbish.

But he'd played along with them, making sure nothing interfered with his release. Just as he'd been careful to keep his nose clean in prison, year after bloody year.

Now he was out, he had plans of his own, but he needed money to carry them out. The do-gooders talked about helping him find employment. He knew what that meant – some dead-end, menial job at minimum wage where he'd be out on his ear the first time he disagreed with the boss. Not for him. He wanted a place of his own, as far away from interfering busybodies as he could get, where he and his family could be self-sufficient. And that took money. Real money, if he was going to have a chance to get on.

He knew how to get his hands onto money quickly. He'd learnt a whole lot of new skills in Barwon, and as soon as he got his bearings, he'd begin working on his personal project.

Then, when he was ready, he'd go and collect Eugenie and his boy.

9

Throughout the following week Geni felt warmed by the support of her friends who made a point of speaking to her every day, either in person or by phone.

Ben was one who never missed an opportunity to make contact.

When no other excuse offered, he simply came knocking on her door. Several times he arrived at her office before she finished work, offering to take Jamie to the park, much to the delight of both Jamie and Bailey, who had faithfully elected to keep him company while he was confined indoors – a confinement which chafed at Jamie, leading more than once to sulky mutterings behind his mother's back.

A happier Jamie meant a happier Geni, who repaid Ben's kindness with dinner invitations. Which led to spine-tingling goodnight kisses.

It was both a pleasure and a frustration since he scrupulously resisted imposing his own needs upon her during this worrying time.

Although it was contrary to his desires, Ben scrupulously let Geni set the pace in their strengthening relationship. A pace she deliberately reined back out of fear of endangering him if she allowed him to get too close, although every day she grew more certain Ben Wright was the man she had been waiting so long to find. The man she had unconsciously been searching for.

These few days were a time of drawing closer, with all her friends, but with Megan in particular. During coffee breaks at work, Geni found herself opening up to Megan more than ever before. No longer was she hiding her true feelings from her best friend. The side benefit of sharing at this deeper level was that she felt a surge of heady optimism. How could she not win through to a happier life with such wonderfully supportive friends?

"You know, Megan," she confided after one such chat session, "I wish I'd talked to you like this years ago, instead of being too ashamed to confide in you. I was afraid if you knew the horrible mistakes I'd made you might not like me anymore."

"Stupid." Megan reached for her in an impulsive hug. "I'm glad you're talking to me now, too. I always had the feeling there was more to you than you let on, but the secret was yours to share or keep, so I very carefully didn't pry. Maybe I should have." This time it was Geni who pulled her friend into a hug, giggling when Megan's baby bump threw her off balance.

~~~~~

The second week began as a repeat of the previous one, but as the days flowed uneventfully by, most of her circle of supporters began unconsciously to relax.

It was inevitable, Geni supposed, that even the most sympathetic people quickly became blasé about the threat hovering like a black storm cloud above her head, since it was virtually impossible to function indefinitely in a state of high alert when nothing happened.

And nothing did happen.

For the first week following Nigel's release, everyone had maintained the strictest security measures, but by the end of the second week, most were backsliding in minor ways. She herself was not entirely immune, as temptation led her into giving in more and more to her desire to spend time in Ben's arms.

At least a dozen times a day she found herself wondering if she had been crying wolf when she insisted she and Jamie were in danger.

Had she started a panic over nothing? In one way she hoped this was the case. The downside though would be the never knowing for certain. The desperate urge to keep looking over her shoulder. Maybe for years to come. She couldn't bear it if she had to go on living like that indefinitely.

If not for Don Matthews' regular updates, negative though they invariably were, and his serious reminders not to let her guard down, she didn't know what she might have done. But if the police sergeant, with all his experience, took the threat seriously, she would too; until he advised her otherwise.

~~~~~

The cricket season was over for the junior players who were already switching their sporting interests over to soccer.

Ben and Alan, their own team not having made it to the finals, were taking soccer registrations and beginning official training on Wednesday nights.

Since most of the children involved were the same ones who had played cricket during the summer, it made sense all round to stick to the same training days, although, in helping Geni out with Jamie, Ben had begun some unofficial training in the afternoons after school as well, thereby giving himself an unassailable excuse to be in the park, standing guard, when Jamie played there after school.

On Saturday, the Junior Soccer League was kickstarting the season with a gala day in Werris Creek, another small town in the region. Geni had agreed to take Jamie unless anything untoward occurred to make it inadvisable to do so. As had become usual practice, she would be including Bailey.

With his best mate along, Jamie was too happy to bother indulging in the usual small boy complaints against her authority.

Meaning, that without having to keep her son amused herself, Geni had more time to pursue her own interests. Which these days seemed to be centred around Ben Wright. Whom she persistently refused to date, or claim publicly as her boyfriend, in spite of the fact they were seeing each other almost daily.

ON the gala day, he had persuaded her to car-club, a move which allowed her to sit back and relax while he did the driving. Although, with Nigel a constant dark presence in the back of her mind, the thought of being without her own transport made her so uncomfortable she had insisted they take her car.

Leaving the known safety of Oxley Crossing felt like stepping out into danger. Ben had protested, since his was the roomier vehicle, but, even knowing she was being unreasonable, Geni had obstinately refused to agree, and he had capitulated. With the two boys on the back seat, she considered herself quite adequately chaperoned, especially with several other cars ahead and behind them all heading to the same destination.

Watching the teams run onto the field for the first game on Saturday, Geni found herself nervously searching for one particular unwelcome face in the crowd of strangers surrounding her. However, after observing for a while, she realised that everyone there was part of their own particular group. There were no men who stood out as being loners.

With that realisation she was able to relax and enjoy the reprieve from having to be constantly on alert. She relaxed even more when Ben stepped away from the coaches' bench for a quick reassuring word.

Leaning in close to her, he clasped her shoulder, speaking quietly.

"I want you to know, Geni. Although it should be perfectly safe here today, I'm not taking any chances. I'll have my eye on Jamie unless he's with you. Goes for all the Oxley Crossing contingent. We watch out for each other's kids at these events. So, relax, Darling, or you'll wear yourself out with nerves."

"Thanks Ben."

Geni felt tension she'd been unaware of ease from her shoulders. As Ben took his place back on the bench, Alan turned to flash a smile at her, so Geni smiled and waved back.

Just then Angie, who had been taking her turn serving in the refreshment kiosk, returned to claim the empty chair beside Geni. After that, her day took on a positively carefree, cheerful aspect.

~~~~~

Arriving home, they found Geoff Tan leaning on the side fence, chatting to Jon. Bailey immediately jumped out, running to tell his father about the goal he'd scored in the last game of the day, and Geni and Ben strolled after him, greeting the two men as they came up to them.

"Geni. Ben. Thank you for looking after this scamp of mine," Geoff said, ruffling his son's hair as he spoke. "Elizabeth and I really appreciate it. Mum would have taken him, but she's not been well lately, and we don't like putting too much extra on her." Geni demurred, and Geoff continued, "Tomorrow my sister is taking Bailey to the movies in Tamworth, and she asked if Jamie would like to go, too."

Tugging on his mother's jacket, Jamie nodded eagerly when Geni glanced his way. Smiling, she gave her approval for the outing. In Tamworth Jamie would be safe; one anonymous child among crowds of others.

"Also," Geoff hadn't finished, "we thought it might be nice to have Jamie sleep over tonight, if that's okay with you, Geni."

This time Jamie couldn't hold his excitement in.

"Yes! I can, can't I, Mum?" Without waiting for her answer, he added, "Thank you Mr Tan. I'll go and get my things. Come on Bailey."

"Sounds like a popular idea, Geoff. I'd better go and check his idea of packing an overnight bag. Does he have time for a shower? Elizabeth won't want him all filthy from a day of soccer."

"Sure thing. I'll wait here. Jon and I hadn't finished discussing the new model Hondas, anyway. Liz and I are considering a new car and I was just asking his opinion."

As Geni followed the boys upstairs to unlock the door, she heard Ben joining the discussion on cars as well. *Men and their cars*, she thought with an indulgent smile. She'd really enjoyed the day, being part of the large group Angie dubbed the 'soccer family', with Ben drifting back to her side whenever he wasn't with the team. She'd asked him to dinner, and now that Jamie wouldn't be there, was eagerly looking forward to having some quiet time with just the two of them. Almost, but not quite, a date. She hadn't changed her mind on that particular issue.

By the time she returned downstairs accompanied by her newly scrubbed son toting his hastily packed bag, the men had unloaded the gear from the car, which Ben had already locked up in the garage for her.

In no time at all, Geoff and the boys had disappeared down the street and Jon had gone inside for his own dinner, leaving her alone with Ben. Holding out her keys, he picked up her's and Jamie's kit and headed up the steps.

"I'll just haul this in for you, Geni. Then I'll be on my way."

"But... I thought you were staying for dinner. It's in the oven, warming up. It'll be ready in five minutes," she protested, her heart plummeting.

"Are you sure?" Ben stopped, looking uncertainly down at her. "If you are, that'd be good. You know how much I hate cooking for myself."

A frown creasing her brow, she followed him slowly back up the steps. Had she misinterpreted Ben's feelings for her, or was he merely being a gentleman? Was he staying for the home-cooked meal, or to be with her? *Grrrr...*

The uncertainty was enough to make her regret her embargo on dating. Gnawing on her bottom lip, she made up her mind to convince him of her feelings, embargo or no embargo. Entering the flat close on Ben's heels, she closed and locked her front door behind them.

The shepherd's pie she had prepared before going out for the day, was done to a turn, so, still unsure of herself after Ben's aborted attempt to leave, she wasted no time serving it up, along with the salad she'd tossed while Jamie showered.

Handing Ben the corkscrew and the bottle of Coonawarra red she'd been saving for a special occasion, she fetched her best wine glasses, wishing she'd thought to acquire candles; which had been surplus to requirements when expecting Jamie to be at the table with them. Background music she could provide, she realised, darting to turn on her ipod, tuning it to a romantic playlist and turning the volume down low.

Neither of them hurried their meal, conversation flowing easily between them. Every time Geni glanced up, which was often, it was to find Ben watching her, his eyes communicating a message she hoped she wasn't misreading. Her heart beat to a faster rhythm, her eyes sparkling as they replied with an encouraging message of their own.

Letting Ben set the pace, Geni cleared the table at the conclusion of the meal, stacking the dishwasher and setting it going.

Later, when Ben stood up to take his leave, just when she was ready to take their relationship to the next level, she found herself rebelling against her self-imposed rules. He never stayed nearly as long as she would like him to, and he always seemed so stiff and proper she had begun to doubt whether the attraction she felt really was mutual after all.

"Thanks for the meal, Darling. It was great," Ben murmured. "I'll be on my way then." However, he seemed in no great hurry, lingering, as if he had something he wanted to say.

Something she might not want to hear?

His actions told her one thing, his words something quite different, confusing Geni again. She'd had enough of it. Nigel had been off the grid since being released, and today she had almost convinced herself it was as Ben believed. He wasn't coming after all. Why shouldn't she take a gamble on finding happiness with Ben? If he still wanted her?

Stepping back, she searched his face for clues. Crossing her fingers behind her back, she dived right in at the deep end.

"Do you really want to go?"

She crossed the room to where he stood with his hand on the knob, about to open the door, and wrapped both arms around his neck, leaning against him so they were in close, full-body contact. She revelled in the feel of hard masculine flesh and bone pressed against her softness, and gazed boldly into his eyes, willing him not to pull away.

"Never. It's just, without Jamie, I don't want to set you up to be the butt of local gossip. I thought that's why you refused to date." He raised his brow in an unspoken question, wondering if he'd somehow got his wires crossed. He had fallen in love with his wife in high school, and lately he'd discovered he hadn't a clue what the current dating rules were. Or if they even applied to a woman with as complicated a past as Geni's.

"It sort of is," she conceded, wrinkling her nose, "but no-one knows you're here tonight. I'd like you to stay." She smiled mistily, taking his hand and leading him back inside.

"Do you mean what I hope you do?"

Ben sure as Hell hoped she did. He hadn't wanted to put any pressure on her after what she'd been through in the past, but he'd been finding it increasingly difficult to perpetually play the gentleman and leave her with no more than a chaste... make that an almost chaste, goodnight kiss, when his body urged him to ask for so much more.

"I want you, Ben," Geni stated, looking him in the eye as she said it. In case she hadn't made herself clear enough, she added, "I want you to make love to me. Tonight."

Well that was pretty clear, but his better nature halted Ben a moment longer.

"Before we take this any further, Geni Darling, I want you to know. I'm in this relationship for the long haul. I love you, and when you're ready, I'll be asking you to marry me."

Geni sucked in a deep breath. Ben couldn't have made his intentions any clearer, could he? And they were so very much the intentions she craved.

Adrenalin spiked, quickening her pulse and respiration. She stared at him, all big eyes and serious, unsmiling face.

"That's good to know, Ben," she replied solemnly, "since I'm pretty sure I love you too. And, when you do ask me to marry you, I'm thinking the answer will most likely be 'Yes'."

Ben couldn't help himself. He lifted her and spun round and round, holding her against his chest while Geni, all doubts cast aside, laughed out loud and hung on as he danced her down the hall. They tumbled onto her bed in a tangle of arms and legs, Ben's mouth claiming hers in a triumphant kiss which went on and on until they were forced to draw back, gasping for air.

"It feels I've been waiting for you forever, Geni Darling." Ben nuzzled her neck, trailing a row of tiny moist kisses up to the sensitive spot behind Geni's ear.

"Since Megan's wedding," she confirmed, sighing with pleasure as his lips found another sensitive point, sending a shiver down her spine. Turning onto her side, she began explorations and experiments of her own, her hands moving over Ben's back, down to his hips, her body writhing against the interestingly large bulge pressing into her abdomen.

"Much more of that, Darling, and we'll be finished before we've properly begun." Ben eased back, finding her lips again, his hands working on buttons and zips, pushing fabric aside to bare her lush body to his hot gaze.

At the same time, Geni reciprocated, disposing of his shirt and eagerly dragging his jeans down over his hips. Which was when they discovered they both still had their shoes on, and fell apart, laughing like loons as they helped each other discard their remaining clothing.

Geni couldn't remember laughter ever being part of lovemaking before and revelled in the joyousness of this time with Ben.

Free at last to feast her eyes upon the sight of his tumescent erection, the laughter stilled, molten desire flaring out from her core along every nerve. Her mouth dried as her fingers reached out to stroke lightly down his length, eliciting a shiver and a muted growl that provoked her into doing it again. Tilting her head back to allow him access to the hollow at the base of her throat, she continued to stroke him, setting up a slow, steady rhythm she hoped was driving him as crazy with desire, as the delightful things he was doing to her breasts with hands and mouth were doing to her.

Her hum of pleasure turned to a whimper when he moved lower, driving her up to a peak. Then over, to begin again, giving her no respite. But Geni wanted to give pleasure every bit as much as she demanded she receive it from her lover. She stepped up the pace of her own ministrations until Ben reared back, reaching for the small packet he'd left ready on her bedside table. Tearing it open with his teeth, he removed the contents, only to have Geni take the condom from him. Rising onto her knees, she knelt in front of him and rolled it smoothly into place, making an erotic caress of her action.

"Now, Love. Come to me."

Her hands drew him down with her and he eased forward, filling her to the hilt with a satisfied groan. He tried to hold himself back, encouraging her to find her release first, but Geni wasn't having that. She forced him to a faster pace, and the two of them raced towards a wild climax, crying out as they were cast into the abyss together.

They lay, spent, in each other's arms, languidly stroking and kissing as their hearts and lungs slowly returned to normal. Except that Ben's didn't do that. Instead, he felt himself hardening again, sooner than he'd thought possible.

"Damn," he muttered, hauling himself up from Geni's arms.

"What's up?" Geni smirked. "Apart from the obvious, that is?" Then she realised he was gathering up the clothes littering the floor beside the bed.

No way.

"You're not planning on leaving already, are you?" Alarmed, she sat up and took hold of his arm. Lowering her voice to a seductive Garbo huskiness, she continued. "I'm afraid I can't possibly allow you to leave without making love to me again. At least once more."

"Nothing I'd like better, Darling, but I wasn't expecting you to take pity on me, and I only had one emergency issue condom in my wallet. More's the pity."

Geni teased him, running her hands over him and pressing herself against him until he couldn't take any more and broke away, hurriedly scrambling from the bed again. A low, sultry chuckle followed him.

"Only one in case of emergencies," she laughed louder. "What kind of piddling emergency were you catering for?" She rolled over as he watched, and groped in the top drawer, bringing out a box of condoms. The large economy sized box. "Isn't it a good thing I provide for full scale emergencies."

She lobbed it towards him, clapping when he caught it one-handed.

"You were pretty sure of yourself, weren't you, Darling?" he queried, peeling the outer wrapping off and helping himself to the contents.

"Yes, I was. Maybe not tonight, but I had no plans on waiting forever. One day very soon I had every intention of triggering an emergency of my own. I made sure *I* was prepared. And aren't you glad I did?"

Ben couldn't deny it. He wasted no time returning to her bed and demonstrating how very glad he was. And when they woke in the middle of the night, he demonstrated it yet again. Only when Eddie Patterson's rooster heralded the dawn, did he once again climb reluctantly from Geni's bed.

"Gotta go this time, Darling," he whispered, answering her mumbled protest. "See you later."

~~~~~

They did see each other later, at the morning church service, after which Ben bought Geni lunch at the café. They sat for quite a while, talking quietly over their coffees, and Ben invited her to spend the afternoon at his house. She was tempted, but with Jamie due home soon, there really wasn't time for the sort of visit she knew Ben hoped for.

"I'm not ready to go public with what you mean to me, Ben. Let's take it slowly a bit longer. See how things go."

"You're not still on about not dating, are you? Not after last night, surely?" Ben asked impatiently.

"Yes. Yes I am." Geni raised a defiant chin. She had time to think her situation over quietly. Rationally.

The outcome being that she felt it might be premature to let her guard down so soon. It might take longer than she'd estimated for Nigel to make his way north and find where she was living.

"I know Nigel hasn't put in an appearance yet, but I still don't know how safe Jamie and I are. He could show up anytime, and lovely as last night was, Ben, it hasn't changed the situation regarding keeping Jamie safe."

And not just Jamie, she added silently. Ben too. He was even more important to her now than when she first made her no-dating stipulation. If Nigel did show up, the only way she could protect Ben was to keep him at a distance. Even if, in doing so, she jeopardised their glorious new relationship. If it was strong enough to last a lifetime, she rationalised, it could survive a brief setback now.

Ben's thoughts were clearly not in sync with hers. There was a decided snap in his voice when he farewelled her at her gate, minutes later, after bringing their lunch to an abrupt end.

He knew he was being unfair to her, but after the last few quiet weeks, he'd reached the stage where he no longer believed Nigel Blount was fool enough to come chasing after Geni to The Crossing.

Convincing Geni her fears were groundless was the problem now. A problem he couldn't see a solution to in the short term.

FINDING MR WRIGHT

10

Monday morning, after tossing and turning restlessly all night, Geni wondered if she was being a complete idiot, continuing to believe Nigel represented a real and present danger. It had already caused a disagreement with Ben which had resulted in her bad night. *Is he right*, she argued with herself, *or should I believe my instincts?*

She wasn't left in doubt for long.

Nausea roiled in her stomach at the sight of Don Matthews propping up the veranda post outside her office when she returned from taking Jamie to school. Lately he'd checked in with her by phone. Appearing in person felt ominous. Especially when he failed to greet her with his customary quick grin.

Today he was frowning and dead serious. Closing the door behind him, he entered on her heels and sat heavily in her visitor's chair. Pushing it back a few inches to accommodate his bulk, he studied Geni, a sombre expression on his face. Her nerves stretched painfully, tempting her to scream at him to get on with it. She let out a pent-up breath when, heaving a sigh, he began.

"This time I've got real news for you, Geni, which is why I'm here in person. Not sure whether to call it good or bad. Point of view, I guess. The thing is, although we still don't know where Blount is, we do know where he's been. And what he's been up to. Seems the bastard... Excuse my language." Geni nodded impatiently, accepting his unnecessary apology as she concurred entirely with his sentiments.

"Blount made too many of the wrong friends and learned too many of the wrong things in prison. Seems he went on a crime spree after getting out. There's been a spate of robberies across Sydney. Service stations, late-night take-away shops and the like. Soft targets. The perpetrator goes in gloved, wearing a balaclava and toting a bloody great knife. Demands the contents of the till, then legs it pretty quick. A couple of witnesses identified his get-away car, which has since been confirmed as stolen. Seems to be working alone, but we're not sure of that. He seems too well organised, considering he's never been to Sydney before."

Geni covered her mouth with her hands, stifling a horrified gasp.

"So far no-one's been injured," Don continued, "but one of those witnesses got a good look at the perp and identified him from Blount's mug shots. CCTV cameras near where Simpson lives picked up Blount in his company a few days ago, but they've both disappeared since. Blount's looking good for all the robberies. Same appearance, same MO, etc. When we checked back there's a trail of similar robberies in Victoria and several towns along the south coast. Looks as if he's been working his way north, building up his kitty as he goes. Stealing cars, using them for a day or two, then ditching them."

Don cleared his throat, clearly uncomfortable sharing this information, and Geni, nodding for him to proceed, appreciated his doing so all the more. Strictly speaking, she knew he didn't have to. Possibly shouldn't, even.

"Saturday night he slipped up. Two customers came in while the robbery was in progress. Knocked the knife out of his hand and pulled the balaclava off. Although he got away from them, cameras definitely confirm Blount as the perpetrator. We have enough to make a strong case against him. As soon as we lay our hands on him we'll put him away for a good long stretch."

Don took off his cap to wipe his brow, then looked sternly at Genie, ashen and trembling, who hadn't said a word since he sat down.

This was worse than anything she'd imagined. Nigel an armed robber!

And he's working his way north, she thought, fighting down the panic threatening to overtake her. *He could be here any time. Maybe he's here already, if he drove through the night.* Why else had he left Victoria unless he really was coming after her? Unless he really was planning on carrying out his threats.

Jamie!

Panic threatened to overwhelm her when her thoughts turned to him. What would happen to her precious baby if Nigel continued to elude the police?

Geni's pulse was racing, her heart stuck in her throat, choking her. She whimpered, unable to help herself, at the same time despising herself for her weakness. She'd be no use to Jamie if she caved in now.

She fought back her terror, digging deep for inner strength.

Don reached across the desk to give her hand a reassuring pat, his calm, matter-of-fact attitude going a long way to steadying her.

"Now don't you go getting all worked up, Geni. You've been doing good so far, so hang in there a bit longer. We don't know for sure Blount is on his way here, you know. The good news is, with confirmation of criminal activity, the police have gone from a watching brief to an active manhunt. With your input, we have a good idea where to look. Chances are, we'll get him sooner rather than later. I just want you to be aware of what's going on. I'll be talking to people around town, putting the word out to look out for him, and I've got my people on full alert. You concentrate on taking care of yourself and that boy of yours."

They talked a few minutes longer, then, the purpose of his visit fulfilled, Don heaved himself out of the chair and let himself out.

Sick to her stomach, Geni locked the front door behind him, wishing Megan was here so she could have a quick cry on her shoulder. However, Megan had gone to Tamworth for a scan and wouldn't be back till late. Geni was on her own.

Mindful of a client due to arrive soon for his appointment, she retreated to her office, where she scrawled 'Please Ring for Admittance' on a sheet of card which she taped to the front door, then went inside, locking it again behind her. It meant she had to get up and open the door for each arriving client, checking through the spyhole first, but if that was what it took to feel safe in her office, then she had no objection to the inconvenience.

Still horribly jittery, she jumped up again and made the rounds of the building, checking to ensure all external windows and doors were secure. She'd barely had time to calm herself before her first client was ringing the doorbell.

As soon as the client left, an interminable time during which Geni had to fight the urge to fidget, struggling to keep her mind on business, she phoned the school to pass on Don's warning. She debated ringing Ben as well as Ms Marsden, but after the uncomfortable way things had been left between them it didn't feel right to interrupt him at work to say, 'I told you so.' Steadier now, she took a moment to think, arriving at what felt to her like a reasonable compromise. She texted an apology, reiterated how wonderful Saturday night had been, and how much she loved him, and finished with a request he ring her during her lunch break if he was free. When she would pass on Don's information.

Ben did better than ring back. As she ushered the last client before lunch out the door, preparing to lock it behind him, Ben came jogging up the steps.

"Ben. I'm so happy to see you..." Geni began, standing back, holding the door open for him.

There was no time for more, because Ben entered, heeling the door shut behind him. In the same motion, he hauled her into his arms, kissing her as if he'd never let her go.

The moment he leaned back, giving them both a chance to catch their breath before they were asphyxiated, she wriggled from his clasp, turning to the door and locking it securely once again.

Ben watched, quizzically raising his brow.

"Are you planning an emergency, Darling?" he murmured, "I'm willing, but time's too short to do justice to the occasion." He grinned, as colour flooded as much of Geni's fair skin as he could see above the neck of her dress. Spending the lunch break making love had been the last thing on her mind, but now he'd planted the idea, she had to admit, it sounded awfully tempting.

"I'd love to," she drawled, rallying fast, "but unfortunately, no. No emergencies today. Not that kind, anyway. Come into the kitchen. I'll make fresh coffee and fill you in. I've had Don Matthews here this morning…" Conveniently, she let him think her text predated Don's visit, considering it unnecessary to ruin his good mood more than she had to. Over a hastily put together salad sandwich, she filled him in.

"I'm glad you came in person instead of phoning, because now you can help me work out the best approach, since Don thinks it now seems quite likely Nigel will actually arrive. Unless the police catch him first."

Ben frowned. It seemed he might have been a bit hasty in writing Nigel Blount off. Instead of working on strategies to handle the bloody man, what he wanted to do was bundle Geni and her son up and hide them away where that bastard wouldn't have a hope in Hell of finding them and keep them safe till the police did their job.

I can just see Geni agreeing to be sidelined, he scoffed to himself. She was too independent to leave the responsibility for her personal safety entirely in other hands. Besides, where could he hide them? Nowhere in The Crossing, that was for sure. All Nigel would have to do would be to ask a question or two and someone would point him in the direction of her friends. Pregnant Megan sprang immediately into his mind.

Nigel hadn't baulked at killing an old woman, so he'd hardly be likely to let Megan, or anyone else, stand in his way.

Geni had been watching the silent argument going on in Ben's head, guessing at what he was thinking. When she saw his shoulders slump in defeat, she finally voiced the ideas she had come up with herself when she and Don Matthews had first conferred on the subject.

"Don thinks it's best if Jamie and I stay in plain sight as long as we continue taking the precautions we've established already. He doesn't say it, but I reckon he sees us as bait, to lure Nigel into the open. It scares me," *and isn't that an understatement,* she thought, bravely attempting a smile to reassure her lover. "But, you know, Ben, I agree with Don."

She laid her hand on his chest, gazing earnestly into his face, mentally compelling his agreement. In her opinion, flushing Nigel out, risky as it was, offered the best chance of a speedy resolution to the whole nasty situation.

"I can see you want to protect us, Ben, and I appreciate your care of us," she continued earnestly. "I'm sure we can summon help in time if he tries to break in, so we're safe behind locked doors, I think, and Ms Marsden has Jamie's security well in hand at the school. That leaves the short time we're out and about in the open. Do you think you could keep on as you've been doing, Ben? Escorting Jamie to and from the park when you have time? I know you're busy, and it's an awful imposition, but Jamie needs a bodyguard we both trust, and I can't imagine trusting anyone more than you."

He'd be Jamie's bodyguard, that went without saying, but Ben didn't like this scheme of Don's to use the Sullivans as bait.

His imagination presented him with too many scenarios of disaster, but Geni remained adamant. Against his better judgement, he agreed, rather than alienate her. When all this was over, he wanted her by his side, alive and unharmed. They were a family, whether Geni realised it or not, and a man took care of his family.

He'd be sticking close as a burr in a fleece, watching out for his woman, as well as her son. Whatever she said.

11

It had been a bit of shitty bit of bad luck, those two heroes coming in when they did, Butch thought sourly. They'd damned well almost nabbed him. In spite of ducking his head to avoid the security camera when his balaclava was yanked off, there was that one moment he wasn't sure of, when he'd had to fight to escape. A boot to the kidneys had made sure that jumped-up wanna-be would think twice before pulling another stunt like that.

Till then he'd had a good run, hitting two or three places just about every night since he got out. The stash he'd put by would last him a good long time if he used it sparingly. Time to quit while he was ahead. It wasn't as if he needed to risk his neck on penny-ante hold-ups any longer. He had a real job now.

The bikie gang Kev had hooked him up with had set him up real good, managing one of their so-called farms on the edge of the border rainforests. It was a sweet deal. In exchange for minding the crop and keeping strangers away, he got paid a decent wage, all expenses, and got this souped-up twin-cab ute carefully disguised to look like an old wreck.

In reality, it could outrun most ordinary police cars. Best of all was a brick house to rival Barwon for security. There was even a lock-up out the back made to look like an old tin shed.

The boss had told him it was for stockpiling the crop when it was harvested, but he reckoned he might be putting it to another use entirely before then. Eugenie wouldn't be escaping from him this time round. Or the kid, either.

Sydney was too hot for him to hang about any longer, so he'd taken a quick run up north to check out the set-up and laid in a few essentials. Made some preparations.

With a place to take them where he wouldn't be interrupted by busybodies, he was ready to collect his wife and kid.

Butch snickered to himself as he turned south onto the New England Highway at a sedate speed unlikely to draw the attention of the Highway Patrol. His natural cunning had prompted him to change his appearance before running after that useless bitch, Eugenie, to the one-horse dump she'd cleared off to. Amazing results he'd had with the stuff he'd picked up from Woolworths the other day. He'd had to take a second look himself, to be sure it was still him. His skin was darker, making him look like some effing wog, and he'd cut and bleached his hair. With respectable new chinos and a checked shirt, his appearance was nothing like it had been in Barwon, except for his height and build. His own mother wouldn't recognise him. If she'd lived past his seventh birthday that was.

Eugenie didn't know what she was in for. Probably wouldn't recognise him even, until it was too late. Unlike him. His eyes strayed to the empty seat beside him where several photos were carelessly scattered.

Thanks to Kev, he knew exactly what they both looked like. Eugenie had always been a tasty armful, he mused, but her figure had ripened since he'd last seen her. He squirmed uncomfortably as his body responded to his erotic daydream of making up for lost time when he got her to himself.

Again, thanks to Kev, who had made a short scouting trip to Oxley Crossing when he found her the second time, he had a whole lot of useful info regarding their current home, work and daily routines. He anticipated no problems at all, locating and making off with them, although he didn't kid himself Eugenie would tamely hop in the ute for him. Not her. Yet another bad habit he'd have to bash out of her. A contemptuous, wolfish grin curled his lips as he imagined administering her first lesson in obedience.

Whistling along to the country music playing on the truck's radio, he plotted his next move. He'd take a day or two to scout around, first. Chances were, he'd need a bolt-hole to stash one of them while he went after the other. Two at a time might be too much of a handful. The kid first, he reckoned; then the woman would come quietly. Once he got them back to the farm, he'd start teaching them the meaning of obedience and respect.

Butch hadn't felt this good in years.

FINDING MR WRIGHT

12

Geni rubbed her hands up and down her arms, shivering again; but not with cold. A jittery feeling, like spiders crawling up her bare arms, had been plaguing her all day, along with a continual urge to look out the window. Searching for… Something. She could almost feel malevolent eyes zeroing in on her, as if she was in someone's crosshairs. It was like nothing she'd ever experienced before.

She shivered again, the creepy feeling starting to make her nauseous. It had eased briefly when Megan came downstairs to have lunch with her, and catch up with some left-over paperwork, but she'd gone up again to rest, leaving her once more alone; prey to the fears she tried hard to rationalise. Officially, Megan was on maternity leave, and shouldn't be in the office at all, but just try telling *her*. Geni smiled. Megan and Jon had asked her to be godmother to their baby, and she couldn't wait to cuddle the little darling when he or she finally made an appearance. But even such happy thoughts didn't distract her from darker ones for long.

Not today.

At five to three, glad to have an excuse to escape the stifling atmosphere of the office, she snatched up her bag and hurried out, locking the door behind her. Rummaging in the depths of the capacious hold-all for her car keys, she trotted down the steps to where she'd parked that morning, right in front of the office door. Where she intended to go on parking till this issue with Nigel was resolved once and for all. Thank goodness it was time to fetch Jamie from school. Sitting around waiting for something to happen was driving her crazy. Even worse, her deteriorating ability to concentrate was having an adverse effect on her work. She'd really wanted to shine; to reward Megan's trust by managing the business, not simply well, but excellently. If today's meagre output represented the new benchmark, she'd be incurring her friend's censure, instead of her praise. Geni made a mental vow to take her unfinished work home and do a midnight oil job of catching up.

Seeing Ben standing outside the front entrance to the school, ostensibly chatting with the teacher supervising the bus queues, but in reality, watching for strangers trying to blend in with the parents picking up their children, perked her mood up no end. He'd been performing this self-imposed extra duty every morning and afternoon this week, his vigilance wonderfully reassuring. She gave him a cheerful wave as she parked and hurried inside. Five minutes later when she returned, Jamie in tow, Ben was standing next to the gate, chatting to a group of children waiting for the late bus. He broke off, crossing to have a word with Jamie.

"Ready for practice later on?" The boy returned a grudging affirmative. He had yet to forgive his former idol for siding with the women in curtailing his freedom.

Ben, perfectly aware of his fall from the pedestal, exchanged a wry smile with Geni.

"I'll be by in about an hour," he informed the youngster, letting his eyes, fixed on the mother's, tacitly transmit a far more personal communication. A pinkening of her cheeks answered him. She ushered Jamie into the back seat and watched him clip his seatbelt in place before driving off with a wave of her fingers for Ben.

~~~~~

"Why do I have to wait for Mr Wright to come and get me," Jamie grumbled, putting his empty mug and plate in the dishwasher in the office kitchen. "I'm not a baby, you know, Mum."

Geni had heard this, or similar complaints, from him every afternoon since inaugurating the stricter protocols. Usually, she was quite patient with him, but after the miserable day she'd had, her tolerance had worn perilously thin.

"You know why, Jamie. I've explained the reasons enough times. Do I really have to go over them again?"

She shut the cupboard door with a bang, making the boy jump. Awash with guilt for so nearly losing her temper, she hugged him, ignoring the way he stiffened, rejecting her affectionate gesture.

"I'm sorry, Love. I understand how frustrating it is for you, not to be able to go outside without an adult, but it's only for a little while longer. Sergeant Matthews thinks all this will likely be settled by this weekend at the latest. Then we can get back to normal."

This time, when she kissed him on the forehead and ruffled his hair, he leaned against her a moment before pulling away.

"Aw, Mum. You don't need to be kissing and hugging me all the time," he protested, but he was smiling again all the same, and he hauled his homework folder out of his backpack and sat down at the table without being prompted.

Geni patted him on the shoulder and returned to her office, determined to work miracles on her mountain of paperwork, no more appointments being scheduled for the late afternoon. However, she'd no sooner sat down than her wayward mind returned to the disturbing sensation of being watched which had been troubling her off and on all day. It was on again now, making her wonder whether or not she should allow Jamie to go to the park later on. *But he'll be with Ben,* she reminded herself. *Ben will keep him safe.*

In a fit of madness, she looked her annoying symptoms up online, and found an off-the-wall site describing her weird feelings so exactly they could have been reading her mind, as an atavistic reaction to impending danger. A warning one was being watched. Targeted. The article went on to cite a whole slew of examples. Enough to make the hairs rise on the back of her neck. God, if that was right... Now she felt worse than ever.

Terrified, if the truth be told.

The phone rang, forcing her to put personal considerations aside. By the time she had finished making an appointment for a face-to-face meeting with her client, she was determined to finish the day on a higher note, with a burst of late afternoon productivity. When her phone pinged an incoming message, she was surprised at how much progress she had made.

She glanced down, a soppy smile banishing her frown.

Ben. He'd finished work, and was on his way, said the simple communication personalised with hearts and flowers emojis.

Discovering Ben possessed a hidden romantic streak was an unexpected pleasure. One she loved to tease him about, just for the fun of seeing him self-consciously colour up. She texted back, returning his romantic sentiments, along with embellishments of her own adding 'I love you,' in plain language at the end, simply for the pleasure of typing the words.

Before returning to her work, she went to tell Jamie and Bailey, whom she'd heard Jamie let in through the back door some time earlier, to pack up. Hearing a beep from outside, the agreed-upon signal heralding Ben's arrival, she went to let him in. About to mention her gut feeling she was being watched, she changed her mind.

With no supporting evidence to back it up, the last thing she wanted was to have Ben thinking she was some crazy, over-emotional flake.

Not when she wanted to appear strong and reliable in his eyes.

So instead, she greeted him with a cheerful smile. With an admonition to the boys to be good, she shooed them all out the door. She had also intended to add an invitation to dinner but decided to wait and see. No way did she intend to set Ben up as a target if she was being watched.

Although she remained in the open doorway, carefully scanning as much of the immediate area as she could, she saw nothing that didn't belong.

The mud-splattered white ute parked a short distance down the street, on a direct line between herself and the park, blended in perfectly. One among several similar vehicles.

Gnawing on her lower lip, a crease once again marring the smooth perfection of her brow, she finally turned away; locking the door and returning to her desk.

~~~~~

Glancing at his watch, Ben called time on the game he'd been refereeing for the group of town children who regularly spent their afternoons playing together in the park. When Billy Porteous came up to him with a question, Jamie, with Bailey a faithful shadow at his heels, ran on ahead.

Ben didn't know what sixth sense alerted him, but he looked up suddenly, seeing a man, a stranger, standing beside a muddy ute, the rear passenger door standing open beside him, and the engine running. He couldn't be certain, but he thought it had been parked there for some time.

When the stranger stepped away from the vehicle, blocking the footpath in front of the two boys, Ben started running. Instinctively, he bellowed a warning.

"RUN! RUN, JAMIE!"

Both boys skidded to a halt.

Abruptly changing direction, they raced across the street, dodging round the back of Fred Lanner's decrepit old Holden slowing to turn into the service station, then straight north along Peel St, Bailey in the lead. Ben hesitated a moment, his eyes tracking both the boys and the stranger.

Until the man he was sure had been planning to intercept them jumped back in the ute, turning with a squeal of rubber as he accelerated, following them. His mind made up, Ben raced in the same direction, legs pumping furiously, giving silent thanks for his fitness.

Half a block ahead of him, the ute turned and braked, riding up over the kerb ahead of the boys, the driver jumping out to once again stand, arms spread, blocking the footpath. There was no doubting his intention now.

Quick-thinking Bailey yelled something to his friend and swerved into the narrow delivery lane alongside his grandfather's supermarket, Jamie right on his heels. The man Ben intuited to be Nigel Blount, took two steps after them, when Ben, closing fast, once again used his commanding sergeant-major roar.

"BLOUNT! STOP! POLICE!"

The police weren't there yet, but it sounded like the right thing to say, and with spectators already gathering, he reckoned one of them would phone for help anyway. Seeing Ben charging full tilt up the footpath mere metres away, Blount spun on his heel and dived back into the ute. Backing onto the roadway, with another squeal of abused tyres and absolutely no regard whatsoever for other traffic, he gunned the motor, racing around the corner and on out of town. Furious his quarry had escaped, Ben stood, hands braced on his thighs, gulping air into tortured lungs.

"Don is coming." Ben looked up, seeing Joseph Tan emerging from the door of his shop. "It was that man our Geni is scared of, wasn't it? I saw and called Don."

"The boys...?"

Ben looked around, not seeing the faces he was seeking in the gathering crowd. They'd raced down the laneway, so he jogged after them, ignoring his wobbly knees. Entering the service yard, he called out, telling them they were safe. It took a moment or two before he spotted two frightened, yet excited, faces peering out from a tangle of bushes growing in the corner between the building and the brick fence bordering the far side of the yard.

"You can come out," he repeated. "It's safe now."

He walked over to help them out of the bushes, surprised to find them clambering out of a gaping hole in the back wall of the building. Bailey, last out, pulled a couple of boards back into place, covering the hole.

"What's down there?" he asked. "You seem to have found a good hiding place."

They both looked down, scuffing the dust with the toes of their sneakers. Finally, Bailey looked up. Reassured that he wasn't in trouble, he blurted out,

"It's the old basement under the store, Mr Wright. Nobody uses it any longer. Gramps keeps it locked, but we found this boarded-up window. It's our secret hideout. You won't tell Gramps, will you?"

"I won't," Ben replied, "but I think you ought to."

He led them round the front, where Don had now arrived.

"I've sent my boys after him," he was saying to Joseph, "but I doubt they'll catch him. He had too much of a headstart."

Don turned to the newcomers, running a visual check of the boys, looking for damage. Seeing none, he huffed his relief.

"What happened, Ben? Joe here only caught the tail end of the action."

"I'll call Geni, first, Don. I don't want her to hear some garbled version from someone else."

Once Geni, pale and fighting back tears, arrived a few minutes later, Don ushered everyone concerned into the police station on the corner of the next block.

"Yasmin, in here." He called on the constable Geni recalled seeing around town on several occasions recently, to join them in his office.

"Yasmin, I've got a job for you." He had Ben repeat the amended description of Blount which Joe corroborated. "If the ute was parked there for a while, as Ben here thinks, then Blount had to have been somewhere not too far away. Maybe having a coffee. Take a look around and see what you can dig up."

That task taken care of, he proceeded to get to the bottom of the incident. At the conclusion of their recital, he sat lost in thought for a bit, until his mobile unit reported in that they had indeed lost their man. Constable Yasmin Sanjoy, however, was more successful.

"Like you thought, Sergeant. He bought coffee and food at Mike Patterson's café down at the service station. Fuelled up as well. That was about four-thirty. Mike Patterson is letting me copy the relevant footage from his security cameras."

When Yasmin Sanjoy arrived back at the station a little later, she had a jubilant bounce in her step.

"Sergeant, I went and looked where the ute was parked, and I found one of Mike's take-away cups in the gutter." Triumphantly, she held up an evidence bag containing the cup. "It might have DNA to prove it was Blount, mightn't it? Then we can add attempted kidnapping to his list of charges when we catch him." Reaching into her pocket, she produced a USB. "Here is the service station security footage. I've looked at it, and there are useable images of both Blount and his ute, although the plates are too muddy to read."

"Well done, Yasmin. I like to see my constables using their brains. Let's have a look, then. We'll see if the bloke you've got is the same one who tried to grab young Jamie, here. He nearly fooled us, changing his appearance like that." Don seemed inclined to take it personally that he hadn't thought of such a trick.

Geni squinted at the image of the smartly dressed blond man, and asked Yasmine to run the short clip again. Straightening up from where she'd been bending down to study the computer screen, she nodded affirmatively.

"That's him. Nigel Blount. The blond hair threw me off, but he hasn't changed the way he walks. His right ankle was broken when he was still at school, and it's left him with that stiff gait." She stepped back and wrapped a protective arm around her son, who snuggled close.

"Thank you, Ben. If you hadn't been so quick to spot him, he might have got away with it." She shuddered, imagining how much worse she'd be feeling now if her ex had succeeded.

"Bailey too, Mum," Jamie whispered, smiling tremulously at his friend. "Bailey helped me escape."

Bailey shyly submitted to being hugged and thanked, then Don started ushering his visitors out.

"I guess I can trust you to see these youngsters home, can't I? My people and I have work to do. Criminals to catch."

~~~~~

"Gramps, I've got something to tell you," Bailey, his hand firmly enclosed in his grandfather's, glanced apologetically at Jamie. "Me and Jamie found a loose board over the window into the basement. We've been playing down there. There's an old ladder we climbed on to get in and out." He hung his head, expecting censure.

"Hmm." Unobserved by the boys, Joe winked at Ben. "Your Daddy used to play hide-and-seek down there. A long time ago now. He fell and hurt himself one day. That is why I keep the door locked. I'd better fix that window. Maybe if you want to play there I can open the door for you, if you ask."

"Can we, Mr Tan?" Jamie was fast recovering from his fright. "It's a great hideout."

Joe chuckled. "Maybe. But now we all go home, eh? Your mother will be worried, Bailey. She will be thinking Sergeant Matthews put you in gaol."

They were all laughing as they separated, heading home in two different directions.

At the bottom of Geni's stairs, Ben hesitated, unsure what she wanted, their status as lovers being too new for him to make assumptions. Until he felt a gentle tug on his hand. Glancing down, he saw Geni smiling at him, and felt his heart soften.

"Dinner?" she asked, her smile turning sultry, offering more than her spoken word.

With Nigel headed for the hills, she needn't fear for Ben's safety tonight. Nor her own. Or Jamie's. And she very definitely felt the need of her man's reassuringly strong arms around her to keep the 'what-ifs' at bay.

Heart thudding almost painfully in his chest, Ben nodded, squeezing her hand. With her son hand in hand on one side and her lover on the other, Geni led her menfolk up the stairs.

"Bath, Jamie," she commanded.

"Aw, Mum. We haven't had dinner yet."

"No, but we're running very late. I'll have food on the table by the time you're out of the shower."

She didn't quite make that deadline, as Ben had something he needed to say first. And then she did, too, although with the meal only needing to be reheated, they didn't keep the starving nine-year-old waiting very much longer than her first estimate. Heading for the kitchen when Jamie scooted down the hallway to the bathroom, Geni looked inquiringly at Ben when he lay his hand on her arm, halting her.

"What's up, Ben?"

"I'm sorry, Darling. I didn't altogether believe Blount would be stupid enough to try anything, so I wasn't as vigilant as I should have been today." He would have said more, only Geni put her fingers over his lips to silence him.

"I know you didn't. But I still believed you'd keep my boy safe, and you didn't let me down. Let it go, Ben. Stop beating yourself up and accept we're none of us perfect."

She rose up on her toes, wrapping her arms round his waist.

"I'm certainly not," she told him.

Pressing herself against his hard-muscled body, she kissed him as she'd been waiting to kiss him since she'd arrived on the scene earlier to find Jamie shaken but safe, Ben's arm holding him protectively close against his side.

With a shaky laugh, she pulled back far enough to whisper, "Later. Now I better do something about that meal."

Only Ben held firm, not releasing her.

It bothered him, knowing he had underestimated Nigel Blount, whom Ben had noticed Don refer to as Butch, much to his consternation. Butch sounded a much more dangerous character than Nigel. And Butch wanted Geni and her son, and today had proved he was prepared to use force to achieve his goal.

Impassioned, voice and face demonstrating his anguish, he said,

"I hate it, Darling, the way you insist on putting yourself and Jamie in the firing line. Can't you leave it to the police from here on?"

Geni opened her mouth, but before she uttered a word, Ben rushed on.

"I could pack you and Jamie up and take you somewhere safe under cover of darkness."

"Where? And for how long? I love you, Ben, but I can't live my life like that – running and hiding whenever things aren't going right. Please don't ask it of me."

When Ben went to renew his argument, she put her fingers across his lips once again, this time stepping back till she was leaning against the kitchen bench, her lips compressed into a determined line.

"Listen to me Ben. I'm not big, or physically powerful, but I'm very strong in other ways. As a single parent I've had to be. Although I'm more than willing to accept help from my friends, no-one makes my decisions for me. I'm not shutting you out. I enlisted you to act as Jamie's bodyguard, remember? I'm relying on you to do something I know I can't. Trusting you with the most precious treasure in my life. I admit, this situation threw me at first, but I've got my act back together again, now. You want me to leave it to the police, and I agree that it's primarily their job. But as long as Don can use my help, in whatever way he wants, he'll have it. I promise you, I'll be guided by him. And I won't take undue risks. Especially with Jamie. I'll be keeping him closer than ever now, no matter how much he complains."

There was not a shred of softness in her expression as she held his gaze. She could hear the metaphorical crackle of thin ice beneath her feet as she laid it on the line; but even if it meant losing the precious future with Ben which she'd so recently set her heart on, she knew in that same heart she would rather lose him than be a mere cipher under his domination. However benevolent and protective it might be. In the Game of Life, she was a team player. Was he? She tried to express herself in terms he'd understand.

"You can stand with me Ben, but not for me."

Ben took in the steely glint in Geni's eyes, the grim expression on her face, and realised he'd unwittingly triggered a make or break situation in their relationship.

He could think of umpteen plausible arguments against her reasoning, but if he overrode her independence, he realised, he would destroy the very spirit which had drawn him to her.

In that fraught moment, he realised something else, as well. He didn't want a meek little clinging vine, or a yes-woman. He wanted this pint-sized Amazon with her fighting spirit. He wanted her standing proudly at his side, the two of them different but equal. Complementary. Even though the very idea of danger threatening her terrified him.

He hadn't realised quite how deeply he'd grown to love her until now, when he came in sight of losing her through his own lack of sensitivity to her needs. Not a mistake he'd be making again, no matter how much it cost him in sleepless worry. Geni's place was at his side, now and forever, and to achieve that goal he'd leash his natural instinct to take charge and let her share control. Although he'd be damned if he'd let her jump in without considering the cost. Or without him guarding her back.

He loved her. Enough, he discovered, to believe in her. To accept her as she truly was. Equally unsmiling, he nodded curtly.

"I'll be beside you, Geni. Every inch of the way. Just don't ever shut me out, will you?"

The tension drained from Geni's body, leaving her giddy with relief. Impulsively, she went up on her toes, pulling his head down to plant another quick kiss on those delectable lips she had just won the right to go on kissing forever.

The unexpected reward reinforced in Ben's mind the wisdom of accepting her ultimatum. He kissed her back. A kiss sealing their pact.

Stepping out of his arms when sounds heralding Jamie's imminent arrival impinged on her awareness, Geni smiled beatifically and set about reheating the meal she had had almost ready to serve when Ben phoned her to come.

For the first few mouthfuls of the lamb ragout which had spent most of the day simmering in the slow-cooker, Jamie ate voraciously, wolfing down his portion. Suddenly, he slowed his attack. Dropping his fork with a clatter, he looked at his mother, mouth trembling in a manner she hadn't seen for several years.

"What is it, Honey," Geni asked gently, reaching out a hand to clasp his.

"I'm scared, Mum. You won't let him get me, will you?" Tears gathered in the boy's eyes. It was only now, when he was safe in his own kitchen with his mother, that it hit home, how very close to disaster he'd been.

"Today was all my fault, wasn't it? Mr Wright said to wait, but I didn't listen. I ran off. Because of me, Bailey and Mr Wright were in danger, too. I'm sorry Mum" Tears were now flowing in earnest, Jamie choking back sobs.

Geni picked him up, big as he was, and sat down with him on her lap, his head pressed against his shoulder. Making inarticulate shushing murmurs, she rocked him till he ran out of tears, then dried his eyes and handed him the tissue to blow his nose.

Ben, who had been feeling particularly helpless, handed him a glass of water. Jamie took a few sips, then put the glass down, but made no move to free himself from his mother's embrace. Judging him ready to listen, Geni chose her words with care.

"You're right, Love," she said, softening what was coming with a gentle kiss, "Your actions did endanger other people. But you know, in the event, nothing very bad did happen, did it?"

She gave him a tiny shake to punctuate her words, pleased when he looked up, almost his usual alert self, although considerably chastened. "You made a mistake, Jamie. Do you remember what we do about mistakes?"

Jamie nodded, and sat up straighter.

"We learn from our mistakes, so the experience isn't wasted," he quoted. He turned to Ben, "I'm sorry, Mr Wright. It won't happen again. Can I phone Bailey, Mum, so I can say sorry to him, too?"

"You can. But finish your dinner first." Judging the crisis over, Geni stood, sitting him back on his chair and resuming her own.

"I agree with your mother, Jamie. Nothing really bad happened, but I'm glad you'll listen to what you're told in future." Ben didn't think it was his place to discipline the boy. Not out of school hours. And the fright he'd had was probably discipline enough.

They continued eating quietly, then once again Jamie put down his knife and fork and, lower lip trembling pitifully again, looked to his mother.

"Do you think I ought to go out to play again tomorrow, Mum? So he'll see me, and try to grab me again, and then Sergeant Matthews can catch him?"

"No I don't."

Geni's emphatic answer came very promptly.

"It's ever so brave of you to suggest it, Jamie, but you and I will leave the catching to the police. In fact, I intend to keep you safe and sound inside until he's caught. Now let's finish this meal before the food is too cold to enjoy." The relieved expression on her son's face told her she'd given the answer he'd been hoping for. Which made her feel like bawling herself.

The meal finally over, Geni sent Jamie off to get ready for bed, and to talk to Bailey and his parents. Alone with Ben, she simply walked into his arms and hung on tight until his large, strong hands rhythmically stroking her back while he whispered words of love and reassurance restored her to a functioning facsimile of her normal self.

"It broke my heart, Ben, listening to him being so scared and brave all at once. If I could have got my hands round Nigel's throat right then, I'd have squeezed so tight…"

"You'd have had to wait your turn. I wish I'd caught up with him this afternoon, but I reckoned it was better to force him to back off, before he got his hands on a hostage." A shudder rippled through Ben's muscular body.

Glancing at the clock, Geni let go and busied herself stacking the dishwasher and, with Ben's help, tidying the kitchen. That task finished, she took him by the hand, leading the way to Jamie's room to say goodnight. When the sleepy boy mumbled "Goodnight Sir," after hugging and kissing his mother, Ben felt his heart turn over in his chest.

Stepping close to the bed, he ruffled the boy's hair.

"Goodnight Son," he replied, hoping it wouldn't be long till he would have the right to claim this boy as his son.

Turning off the lights as she went, Geni led the way to her bedroom. She wanted the comfort of Ben's body, his love, and saw no reason to wait any longer. The loving that ensued was slow, tender, comforting, and, when neither could wait another moment, wholly fulfilling.

Geni's last thought as she fell asleep in Ben's arms, one small hand resting possessively over his heart, was that she had come home. That she was safe.

FINDING MR WRIGHT

13

Just my luck that big bloke playing soccer with the kids saw what I was up too and raised the alarm.

Try as he would, Butch couldn't pinpoint where he'd gone wrong. Another couple of steps and he'd have had the kid in the ute and have made his getaway. He nearly pulled it off on the second try, too. Except the kid, already spooked, was too quick.

Then the same interfering bloody arsehole started shouting for the police and the nosy parkers came crawling out of the woodwork. He'd made it to safety by the skin of his teeth.

The original plan had been to stash the kid in the old shed he'd sussed out down a side track a bit out of town, then phone that bitch Eugenie and convince her to meet him without letting on to the police. All nice and quiet, like.

Then home to the farm where he'd made the necessary arrangements to secure them long-term.

Where he'd teach them the meaning of obedience and see to it his bitch of a wife learned her place.

He'd bet it was down to her, that bloke being so on the ball. She must have recruited him to keep an eye on the kid.

His temper seethed, and he kicked out savagely at the bedroll he'd spread on the floor. The empty bedroll which ought to have been wrapped around the trussed-up kid.

That was the plan then.

Now he needed to rethink the whole damn thing.

It was a bloody nuisance, but no matter how much thought he gave the matter, now he'd lost the element of surprise, he couldn't see his way clear to snatch both of them without getting caught. So. One or the other. Stuffing his face on the two ham and salad rolls he'd picked up at the café that afternoon, he considered his options.

There was really only the one. A bloody slim one at that. Then he'd have to wait months for the uproar to die down and people to get careless, before he'd be able to return for another go at finishing the job.

Butch bared his teeth in a feral snarl.

With the police on the lookout, he'd only get one chance. He'd have to make his move so fast they wouldn't even know he'd been there. Decision made, he sorted out the gear he'd need and got everything ready, then curled up in the abused bedroll and slept. Deep and dreamlessly, like a man with a clear conscience.

14

Geni woke with a smile on her lips. Stretching luxuriously, she recalled making love with Ben a second time during the night, when they both roused and reached for each other. If possible, the second time had been sweeter and more satisfying than the first. She'd heard Ben stirring shortly before dawn. When he kissed her goodbye as he left, she'd been tempted to tell him to stay.

Then she recalled the events of the afternoon before and let him go. If Nigel... Butch, as he was apparently now known, was watching, she didn't want him seeing her lover leaving her home. Didn't want his evil attentions targeted on her Ben.

Sometimes she'd found herself wondering if her memories were painting Nigel blacker than he actually was, but recent events were proving her all too correct in her assessment of his character. If anything, she had underestimated his capacity for evil.

She shivered, rubbing her hands over the goosebumps which had sprung to life on her arms.

Maybe they'd seen the last of him. Butch. She frowned, her soft mood totally dissipated now as her inner warrior shouldered the passionate lover in her aside.

The Nigel she'd known had scared her, but not nearly as much as Butch, the hardened criminal he'd metamorphosed into during his years in prison, did. Somehow, she couldn't convince herself they'd seen the last of him. A one-track mind was one of his personal traits which she recalled very clearly. She thought long and hard, trying to second-guess him.

Would he come after Jamie again? *Yes*, she nodded to herself. *He'll be back*.

On consideration, Geni decided Jamie would be out of Butch's reach at school, safer than with her, if Butch broke into the office.

She would call on Jon to stand guard while she got her son into the car to deliver him there. And Ben, that wonderful man she'd been so fortunate to find, would be waiting in the school car park to resume his role of bodyguard. She'd arrange similar precautions in the afternoon.

Nigel Blount wouldn't be getting his cruel hands on Jamie. He could claim paternity as loudly as he liked; it took more than blood to make a father, and he failed every test.

Actually, she thought, his recent actions would disqualify him for paternal rights if they ended up facing off in court. There was always a silver lining; if you looked hard enough.

~~~~~

The school run went exactly according to Geni's plan.

Jon, alerted by a quick phone call, wandered out to survey the street and check Geni's car. Satisfied, he whistled, which brought Trixie on the run from the back garden and the Sullivans from upstairs. He saw them into the car and waved them off, returning to the garage where he disappeared under the hood of Joey Lambert's beat-up old Holden station wagon, replacing the alternator.

At the other end, delivering Jamie to his classroom went as smoothly as usual. Together, Ben and Ms Marsden ran a tight ship. Now, even more than usual, there was no opportunity for an unauthorised person to endanger any child under their jurisdiction. As well as having a quick word with Mrs Johnson and then Ms Marsden, Geni had to run the gauntlet of well-meaning friends wanting to get to the bottom of the wild stories circulating round town. The result being that she was later than usual getting back to the office. Her preferred parking spot directly in front of the door was occupied, and she had to make do with one a little further away.

Jon, who'd been keeping an eye out for her, stepped onto the footpath, wiping his hands on an oil-stained rag.

"Hey Geni," he called, giving a wave. "Everything okay at school?"

"Perfect Jon. Thanks for standing watch. I'm late. Gotta run."

Returning Jon's wave, Geni jogged down the footpath and straight up the steps, eyes down, intent on fishing the keys out of her bag. Her mind already focused on work, she didn't notice the very ordinary dirty white ute angle parked between the bank manager's dark blue Taurus and another, almost identical, white ute.

Although the driver was nowhere to be seen, the driver's door stood slightly ajar and the perfectly tuned engine idled softly.

Neither had Jon noticed it, obscured as it was by other vehicles.

The only witness to what happened next was Mandy Roberts, an early customer emerging from the bank. Mandy's piercing scream brought Jon, still standing on the footpath outside the garage while he watched Geni trot up the steps, at the run. Just in time to see Butch Blount toss Geni's inert body into the uncovered bed of the ute, jump into the driver's seat, and speed off down Bridge Street, over the Morgan's Creek bridge, and out of sight along the Tamworth road.

~~~~~

"Ben! Blount's got Geni!" Jon's bald statement over the phone brought Ben, his stomach dropping alarmingly, out of his chair in a bound.

"What? How? She was just here. Perfectly alright."

"I'll explain later. The police are on it and Alan and I are going after her in the SES truck. If you want in, grab your kit and get down to the assembly point pronto. Change in the truck."

Before Jon finished speaking, Ben was hauling the kitbag containing his State Emergency Services uniform out from the storeroom, phone up to his ear in the other hand.

"I'm in," In spite of his ashen pallor, his voice was grim. Composed. "On my way," he added, ending the call without further discussion.

As Jon said, there'd be time for explanations later. Shoving the phone into the kitbag, he snatched up his car keys and ran, calling out a terse, "SES callout," to his secretary as he dashed past her desk on his way out. Sandra Campbell, who'd worked there since long before his arrival in The Crossing, knew the routine. Sometimes Ben felt she could run the school quite efficiently without him. But none of that mattered to him at that moment.

All that mattered was Geni. His heart thudded painfully in his tight chest, as he raced towards the carpark.

With as little regard for other road users as Blount had shown scant minutes earlier, Ben floored the accelerator and raced the short distance to the Emergency Assembly area on the block just past Patterson's garage.

Jon and Alan, already in their bright orange overalls, jumped into the front seats of the truck which was permanently equipped to handle any situation in which they might be called upon to render assistance. Ben tossed his bag into the back seat, following it in without a word spoken. Alan threw the truck in gear and moved out before Ben had the door shut.

"Fill me in," he demanded, voice muffled as he began scrambling out of his clothes and into his own orange overalls and heavy boots, not the easiest of exercises in the confined space.

"I'm sorry. It was my fault. I should have walked her in," Jon began.

"It's Blount's fault, so don't waste time apologising. Tell me what happened."

"Right."

Jon swallowed hard, guilt still searing his gut. Whatever anyone said, he'd been responsible for Geni's safety, and he'd failed her. He should have gone down the footpath to where she parked and escorted her to the door. Watching from fifty metres away wasn't good enough. As events had proven.

"The bastard had snuck in and was hiding in that dark corner behind the pillar on the end of the veranda. He grabbed her when she went to open the door to her office. Injected her with something really fast-acting, because she never had time to shout, even. Mandy Roberts did that. She saw the whole thing as she exited the bank at the other end of the veranda and screamed blue murder."

Jon, hoping his careless choice of words wasn't prophetic, gulped in a fresh breath and gabbled on, trying to be as succinct as possible.

"He picked Geni up and tossed her into the bed of his ute. It was behind a row of parked vehicles, and I missed it."

Another failing he was kicking himself over.

"Sped out across the bridge, as if he's heading for Tamworth. I called Don, and he's got his boys onto it."

Just then, the radio, already tuned to the police channel, crackled into life.

"Highway Patrol roadblock in place. Ready when he gets here. Backup on the way. Over."

"Both cars from Oxley Crossing approaching from this side. Over."

"That last was Don," Alan muttered. "Sounds as if they're trying to get him before the crossroads. Makes sense. If he gets past there, he's got a choice of roads. Could end up anywhere."

"So, where do we fit in? Why the SES truck?" Ben asked.

His mind was still grappling with the confusing events. He couldn't believe how fast his life had been turned upside down at the very moment he was most hopeful of achieving long-lasting happiness.

"Oh, well."

Alan sounded a trifle sheepish beneath the hard edge. He'd overstepped his authority in taking matters into his own hands. Even though he was SES captain, this use of the truck was completely unauthorised, but he'd worry about that later.

"You know, Ben. As civilians there's no way the police will give us a look-in. As SES, we have some sort of official standing. They're used to working with us in rescue situations. I reckon we keep clear of them but be ready to give a hand if the opportunity presents itself."

"And we'll be there for Geni when they get her back. I see."

After that exchange, there was silence, except for the police chatter over the radio as the different units maintained contact with each other.

"Suspect vehicle approaching. Over."

Ben recognised the voice of the officer manning the roadblock at the crossroads. He tensed, sitting forward on the edge of his seat, ears straining above the combination of engine noise and static for more details.

"Shit! Saw us and is turning round. Heading back your way, Don. Over."

"Highway Patrol in pursuit. Over."

That was the backup team at the roadblock. Sirens screaming over the airwaves set Ben's gritted teeth on edge. The frustration was killing him. Every nerve in his body strained towards action, and he was stuck here. A useless bystander, while God only knew what was happening to the woman he loved.

~~~~~

Shit! Shit! Shit!"

In time with his expletives, Butch thumped the steering wheel with his fist.

So bloody close. How in Hell did the bloody Highway Patrol arrive so fast?

He'd had his escape perfectly planned. That damned crossroad shouldn't have been blocked off. He should have sailed through without any trouble, then a few quick direction changes on the backroads, a brief stop to deal more efficiently with his wife, he glanced over his shoulder momentarily at the oversize sports bag and other gear he'd lifted from the locker room under the grandstand last night, then fixed his eyes on the road again.

He was pushing the ute to its very surprising limits and couldn't afford to be distracted. The Highway Patrol chaser was sticking to him like a flea on a dog, and he knew the local plods would have stirred themselves into action by now.

He couldn't afford to forget them. They would be somewhere up ahead. If he could get to the bypass round the town first, then he'd hit the forest trails and lose his tail when it got too rough for pursuit. With his four-wheel-drive capability he'd have no trouble.

His mental clock was ticking in his head. The shot of ketamine he'd given Eugenie to knock her out would be starting to wear off shortly. He had to find somewhere to deal with her before she recovered her strength.

He thumped the wheel again. There were too many sodding details to keep track of.

Maybe Kev was right when he said I oughta write her off.

~~~~~

"Madden. Ffolkes." – Don again – "Block the road and we'll trap him between us. Over."

"All set up Sarg," came the response a few moments later. "We're inside the cutting. No way he can get past us here. Over."

Alan caught up to Don Matthews's 4WD police truck at the entrance to the cutting, cruising to a stop behind him. Young Jimmy Ffolkes was jogging back to the patrol car after setting out his 'Road Closed' signs to stop other traffic getting in the way.

"Damn idiots."

Alan thumped the steering wheel, then jumped out and marched up to Don, Jon and Ben hard on his heels.

"Don. Let us through. He can see you here as he comes down the straight. The turnoff to Rainbow Falls is just a hundred metres ahead. You don't want him dodging down there. We'll block it and cut him off from there. With you here and the Highway Patrol behind, we'll have him boxed in."

"Right. My constables are new. Lack of local knowledge. But I'll go forward to block the turnoff. You lot," he pointed an admonishing finger at the trio, "keep out of our way."

He ran back to his truck, shouting at Constable Madden to let him past.

"Bloody Hell!"

"He's too late, isn't he?"

The breath hissed from between Ben's lips, his hands clenching impotently at his side.

Blount, approaching faster than his ute should be capable of going, had just entered the long straight section of road ahead of them, the Highway Patrol, lights flashing and siren wailing, hard on his tail. Seeing the roadblock ahead, he hit the brakes, and, fish-tailing wildly, shot down the side road to the falls.

The three police vehicles fell into line behind him, their visibility instantly reduced to nothing by the billowing clouds of dust rising from the gravel road.

Ben led the charge back to the SES truck, Alan and Jon half a gasp behind him.

Thinking they'd do as previously and follow the police lead, he was stunned when Alan floored the accelerator, ignoring the turnoff to race ahead down the main road.

"What the..." he began, turning in his seat to look back at where the police had chased after Blount towards Rainbow Falls.

"Local knowledge," Alan answered, yelling to be heard over the noise of the labouring engine.

"This is my backyard out here. There's a back road to the Falls using a fire trail through the Lanner property. Comes out up the hill above the lip of the falls. If Blount gets on it he could get clean away."

Ben recalled that 'Morgan's Run', Alan's family property lay across the creek from Rainbow Falls. He tried to visualise the topographical maps the SES used but couldn't bring this area clearly to mind.

"Better hang on," Alan advised, several minutes later, swinging the wheel to avoid the worst of the potholes on the rutted farm track. "When we turn onto the fire trail it's going to get rough."

"Rougher than this, you mean?" Jon latched onto the grab handle as he was flung sideways against the passenger door.

Alan's reply was a grimly amused "Hah!" as he concentrated on manoeuvring the bulky vehicle along the wheel-ruts marking the narrow passage snaking through forested land closely bordered by a steep drop-off to Morgan's Creek on their right.

They burst out from the shadowed track into a clearing beside the creek at the same time as Blount's ute entered it from the other side, Don Matthews cresting the hill behind him. The wheel-ruts ran straight into the water, emerging on the other side of the creek.

"Shit!"

Alan put his foot down, desperately trying to cut the ute off before it entered the water, but he was too late.

"The bloody idiot! Didn't he see the signs? He can't cross here, it's too deep. The ford was washed out in a flood a couple of years back. Before your time."

Alan thumped the wheel, frustrated at failing in his goal. Of the three of them, he was the only one who understood how dangerous it was to attempt a crossing so close to the top of Rainbow Falls where the creek narrowed, funnelling the water into a fast, deep channel cascading over and around huge boulders, finally leaping out over the abyss, creating the perpetual rainbows which gave the falls their picturesque name.

"But... If he can't cross? We'll have got him. Won't we?"

Alan snarled at Jon's confusion, and jumped out to stride across and join Don.

Another who knew the score, he stood, arms akimbo, watching Blount's attempt at escape and issuing orders to his colleagues who, without the luxury of four-wheel-drive, had halted at the base of the falls to await orders. Ben and Jon ran to the water's edge, staring after the ute pitching and lurching its way towards freedom.

"Geni!"

Ben yelled, so desperate he waded into the swiftly flowing stream. She was so close, no more than five metres away, and the ute had slowed to a lurching crawl. If he could just reach her in time... A strong hand grabbed a fistful of his overalls and hauled him back. He swung round, hands raised aggressively.

~~~~~

Geni groaned and dry-retched, then was flung down again as she tried to sit up. She'd begun to come round several minutes ago, but her body refused to respond properly. Her muscles remained frozen. Useless.

She could tell they were speeding, then had come that wild turn when she'd tried to sit up. Now the road was bumpier, bouncing her around like a sack of potatoes, dust billowing up behind them. They changed direction again, and she copped a faceful of red dust, making her cough.

Her muscles might be out of action, but her brain was starting to tick over quite nicely. She took stock of the situation, striving to glean as much information as she could.

Realising her limbs were free, she began making plans. She wasn't going to sit here meekly and let Nigel do as he liked with her. She'd go down fighting. Take him with her if she could. If she could get out… They were going too fast at the moment, but if he slowed down…

Sirens.

They'd been screaming in the distance for a while, she realised. She struggled to look out from the back of the ute. Nothing to see through the thick dust, but the noise was ear-piercing. That meant there were police cars right behind them. She wasn't alone. The knowledge that help was at hand boosted her resolution to escape.

Suddenly she was flung down again, tumbling helplessly to slam up against the tail-gate as the ute began climbing. The speed slowed, but not enough.

The ute braked hard. This time she fell forward, banging her head against the back of the cab and almost knocking herself out. Almost immediately it spun ninety degrees and moved forward, pitching and yawing like a boat in rough seas; much more slowly than before.

Geni struggled to sit up again. At this much slower speed she might have a chance to scramble out. It would be worth a broken arm or a sprained ankle, and the police would be there to stop Nigel grabbing her again.

"Geni!"

She could swear Ben had just called her name, but how could that be? She must have hit her head harder than she thought.

~~~~~

"Jon! Ropes and harness!" Alan shouted, shaking Ben out of his blind rage.

"He won't make it across. We'll need safety gear to reach him wherever he ends up and bring Geni back. Blount too, I suppose."

"He's lost it!"

Intent on their confrontation, they'd taken their eyes off the ute. At Don's shout, they looked back to see it slew sideways into a deep hole. Engine flooded and wheels losing traction, it was totally at the mercy of the water, the fast running stream dragging it downstream from the defunct crossing.

As they watched, Geni's head rose above the rim of the tray-back, her hands clutching at the edge, terrified eyes pleading for help.

"Geni! Stay down!" Don bellowed, using exaggerated hand signals to back up his words. He huffed his relief when she subsided onto the floor, hands fastened in a death-grip on the side of the tray.

The men ran along the bank, keeping pace with the helpless ute wallowing its haphazard way towards the head of the falls, bouncing off the huge boulders which were strewn randomly along the creek-bed.

Ben's heart had leapt joyfully at that first glimpse of Geni's blonde head peeping from where Blount had flung her. Whatever he'd used must be wearing off. A second later, he saw her danger as clearly as Don had. Even a strong swimmer would be in trouble in the deep, fast-flowing water. And with the falls so close...

Doing a slow, almost graceful pirouette in the middle of the creek, the ute wedged itself between two banks of rock jutting up above the water.

And there it hung, being pounded on by the cascading flood, but unable to go anywhere.

Jon, having seen what was happening, had driven the SES truck along the bank, coming to a stop with the nose pointing towards the water. He leapt out and began hooking a heavy cable to the winch at the front.

Seeing what he was about, the others raced to help, the three of them a practised team, each automatically doing what they'd trained for. Don stood back, letting them get on with it, keeping his eyes on the ute. On Geni who still peered fearfully over the tailgate. And on Blount, who seemed to be struggling to climb out the window of the cab.

"Blount's trying to make a run for it," he shouted, running out onto the rock platform jutting into the stream. They all halted, watching as the man they were hunting struggled out through the downstream window of the ute.

At first it looked as if he might succeed in scrambling onto the rocks, using the bulk of the stalled ute to save him from being washed away. Until he spotted Don edging forward, ready to bring him down as soon as he was within reach. Distracted, he lost his footing, skidding on the slippery, slime-covered rocks.

Afterwards, when called upon for official statements, none of the four men could say with certainty whether Blount's hands had slipped or he'd let go.

Either way, the result was the same. He fell back into the water and was carried away towards the falls, bouncing off rocks and being submerged then resurfacing several times before disappearing from sight.

Geni's wordless scream snapped Ben out of his trance. She sat in the bed of the ute, hands covering the lower half of her face, eyes fixed on the spot they'd seen Blount's body disappear over the lip of Rainbow Falls.

"Stay still Geni," he yelled, struggling to make himself heard over the roar of the water.

"I'm coming to get you." He donned the harness, checking the connection to the winch, then wrapped a second cable over his shoulder.

With Alan operating the winch, and the other two guiding the cable away from snags, Ben eased into the water and let it carry him till he reached the ute.

Holding onto its side, he unwound the second cable. Passing it up to Geni, he instructed her how to put on the harness attached to the end of it, then helped her into the water where he clutched her tightly against his chest. She wouldn't be needing the fail-safe harness she'd struggled into. No way would he release his grip on her slender, precious person. Bending his head, he allowed himself one quick, very quick, kiss before signalling they were ready to be winched to safety.

Eager hands hauled the two of them from the water, backslapping and hugs a joyous release from the unrelenting tension of the last hour or so. Astounded, Ben glanced a second time at his watch, barely able to believe the several lifetimes he'd lived through since Jon's phone call had passed so quickly. Back at school it was barely morning recess. He reached into the truck locker for towels. Wrapping one round Geni, he started rubbing her hair dry with another, although he didn't think the shivers running through her body were all down to being cold and wet. If asked, he'd have to admit to being a bit shaky himself.

Don had been on his radio, talking to the rest of his team. Now he returned, walking heavily, his solemn face foreshadowing his news. He warmed Geni's hands between his large paws, offering what comfort he could.

"Alex Madden says they fished Blount's body out of the pool down below. He'd bashed his head in on the rocks, and they reckon he was probably dead before he went over. The autopsy will tell us for sure."

Tears began trickling down Geni's cheeks, and Ben pulled her gently against his shoulder, folding her within the shelter of his arms.

The trickle became a flood, and sobs wracked her body. But the storm didn't last long. Easing back, she looked round the circle of strong men who'd restored her faith in the male of the species, ending with the one who'd taught her to trust again. To love without reservation. Her mouth wouldn't form a smile yet, her muscles were still not working properly from whatever Nigel had injected her with, but she smiled and smiled on the inside.

"I'm alright," she mumbled through stiff lips. "So relieved it's all over, though I never wished him dead." She leaned back against Ben's chest, clutching the damp towel around her shoulders.

"Does Jamie know? About me?"

"No." Ben wasn't one hundred percent sure of his answer's veracity, but he very much doubted Carolyn Marsden would have let anyone talk to him about the morning's events yet.

"Can I phone him? Please?" She looked at Ben as she asked, so he gently set her aside and went to retrieve his phone from the truck. He had a few words with Carolyn himself before walking over to hand the phone to Geni.

"Here you go. I've got Carolyn Marsden on the line for you."

While the men gave her privacy, stowing the equipment they'd used, and Don liaised with his seniors in the Department, Geni talked to her son, explaining what had happened and reassuring him the crisis was really over.

"There's nothing wrong with me a shower and dry clothes won't fix," she assured him, not for the first time.

"I'll be at the school to talk to you in person, just as soon as I can, Jamie love, and you'll see for yourself."

Finally ending the call, she stood on shaky legs and tottered over to the truck, steadying herself against the front roo bar. Ben was immediately at her side, a supporting arm round her waist.

"Don," he called, "We'll get a move on now. Geni needs to get home."

Don hurried across.

"That's okay, but I need official statements from all of you. Especially you, Lass. The Powers That Be demand a full accounting. Pop into the station sometime over the next day or so. In the meantime, Constable Yasmin Sanjoy, who's been manning the station on her own all morning, has been doing a bit of research into the contents of the syringe we found back where you were grabbed, Geni. Seems it was most likely ketamine, which ties in with a break-in from a vet supply outlet last week. If that's it, the effects will wear off completely sometime soon, depending on how much he used. Although I still want you to report to Doc Rogers as soon as you've cleaned up. I won't be comfortable till you're given a clean bill of health."

Relief surged through Geni, and she let herself slump in Ben's arms. It had been worrying her that her poor muscle control and difficulty articulating might be permanent. Feeling the tension ease from Ben's body, she knew she wasn't the only one who'd been concerned.

There was nothing more to keep the civilian contingent any longer, so they piled into the truck for the drive back to town. At a considerably slower pace than their mad dash to rescue Geni.

FINDING MR WRIGHT

15

"Here we are, Geni." Alan pulled the truck over outside Geni's flat.

Ben jumped out first, then helped her descend to the footpath. He was rudely jostled aside when Megan came running from the office next door. Jon had phoned her several times during the morning, keeping her up-to-date with developments, and she had been at the window, watching for their arrival for the last ten minutes.

"Oh. My. God. Geni," she exclaimed, patting her friend down, checking for injuries, "just look at you. You're sopping wet and filthy and covered in bruises. What did that animal do to you?"

Without Nigel Blount there in person for her to vent her anxiety upon, she did the next best thing. She thumped her husband in the arm, not bothering to pull her punches. "You men were supposed to be looking after her," she accused. "How could you let this happen?" Tears were flowing, rapidly building up to a flood, when she turned on Alan, next closest to her, fists clenched to administer more punishment.

Alan wasn't having that. He caught her fists in his large hands and held them immobile against his chest.

"I'll allow a thump from Mum or Angie. Maybe Eddie. But you don't make the cut, Meggie. Give over."

"Oh Hell! I'm sorry Alan. Jon, you know I didn't mean it. I know you did everything anyone could have, and you've brought my girlfriend back to me, even if she's not in pristine condition." Megan was by now sobbing in earnest.

Jon was patting her on the back and making ineffectual murmurs she couldn't hear over the noise of her own wails. Alan and Ben, eyeing her as if she was a dangerous new species, were edging away to a safe distance. Worried that all this excessive emotion was bad for the baby, Geni stepped in. Taking Megan's face between her hands, she spoke loudly. Firmly. With a take-no-prisoners deliberation.

"Stop that noise! Right now, Megan! Stop it!" Her voice penetrated her friend's hysteria, and, to her amazement, the ruckus stopped. Instantly. Megan gaped at her, then, shutting her mouth with a snap, she blushed a fiery red. Redder than she already was.

"What am I doing? Oh Geni, you're the one who was kidnapped, drugged and nearly drowned and I'm carrying on like a two-bob fool. You ought to have slapped me one."

"If yelling at you hadn't worked, that was next." Geni giggled, then Megan joined in. Their uncontrolled mirth didn't quite rate as hysteria, but it wasn't far off.

By this time a crowd had gathered, everyone eager to hear the full story.

Eddie Patterson wriggled her way through, no-one contesting her right to a front-row position. Neither did anyone contest her right to take charge.

"Jon," she started with the, to her, most serious need.

"Take Megan inside and sit her down with a nice cup of herbal tea. Feet up for at least half an hour, Meggie dear."

She looked around for her next target.

"Geni. Here's your handbag, Dear. Megan picked it up off the veranda where you dropped it. Your keys are inside." She thrust the bag into Geni's hands, accompanying it with a kiss on the cheek.

"Ben Wright, make yourself useful. Take Geni home and see that she gets a hot shower and dry clothes. A cup of tea and a sandwich while she rests would be a good idea, too. Off you go."

She flapped her hands at them as if shooing a flock of chooks.

Geni returned the kiss, adding a hug, then turned to Ben who winked and put an arm around her to help her up the stairs.

Not that she needed help, but it felt nice, so she took advantage, leaning against him. Which caused an immediate tightening of his supportive half-embrace. She handed him the keys and while he unlocked her door, she turned to listen to Eddie, still organising everyone below.

"Now, Alan dear. Tell us quickly what happened so we can all go about our business, and you can put that truck back where it belongs."

Alan's voice giving an expurgated version of the morning's happenings was the last thing she heard as Ben shut the door quietly behind her.

"You know, Darling," she commented mildly, observing him turning the key in the lock. "We don't need to lock the place up like Fort Knox any longer."

"Maybe not, but I'd rather not have any of that lot out there bursting in on us unannounced."

"Oh," Geni whispered, wrapping her arms around him when he lowered his head to claim her lips. "I'm not sure this is what Eddie intended, but I approve wholeheartedly."

The first kiss led to more. Hungry, voracious kisses that neither of them could get enough of. Two pairs of hands were everywhere, stroking, kneading and tearing at their clothes.

"Help me get these wet things off," Geni panted, wrestling Ben's overalls off him. "I want to make love with you. Now." She demanded, urging him to hurry.

"You're sure?"

"Never surer."

When his boots got tangled up in his overalls, threatening to trip him, they both laughed, and worked together to free him. Unencumbered at last, he picked her up and strode into her bedroom. Dropping her onto the bed, he stripped the last of her garments from her, tossing them aside. Geni pulled him down on top of her, mouth and hands urging him on. It was all speed. Lightning fast. All fiery passion with no time for gentleness or finesse. More about reaffirming life than about love, though love featured prominently in the mix, too.

Their wildness burned away the old fears which had haunted them both for weeks, and the sharp, new terrors of the morning. They had survived, and their desperate loving reaffirmed that they were alive. That they had a future.

They drove each other on, racing and straining for completion. Gasping to draw breath into air-starved lungs. Slick with sweat, they took the final leap together, Ben collapsing onto Geni's body, sprawled bonelessly beneath him.

He felt he'd never have the strength to move again, but somewhere in the far reaches of his consciousness, he realised he must be squashing her. He pushed himself up and rolled onto his back, drawing her down onto his shoulder, his arm holding her against him.

"Mmmm," she purred. "Thank you Darling. I needed you. I'll always need you, but today was different, and you gave me exactly what I needed."

"The need was mutual, Geni my love. And I'll always need you, too. I love you. Forever."

He kissed her. Softly. Gently.

And she kissed him back. Equally softly. Equally gently. The kisses interspersed with heartfelt declarations of their love, with no holding back. No reservations. They were more open and honest with each other than ever before, and inevitably they made love again.

Softly. Gently. Tenderly.

With none of the wild frenzy of the first time. Once again, it was exactly what they both needed. Their shared climax came slowly, building and building inside them without urgency.

When they cried out, together, the explosion of ecstasy reverberated endlessly, leaving them as totally spent as the first time. They slept in each other's arms. Deep, dreamless, healing sleep.

They didn't sleep for long, but they both woke refreshed and full of energy.

Turning her head, Geni caught sight of the clock on the bedside cabinet, and gasped. Sitting bolt upright, she threw her legs over the side of the bed.

"Darling, what's wrong?" Ben murmured sleepily, reaching to pull her back down beside him.

"Come on, Ben. We don't have time for that, much as I'd like to make love with you again. Get up. It's almost time for me to fetch Jamie. I have to shower and get dressed. Hurry up."

Galvanised into action, they rushed into the bathroom. When Ben saw Geni's body in full light for the first time since they'd arrived home, he was shocked.

"My God, Geni. You're bruised all over. I must have hurt you something awful. I probably added to the tally," he added guiltily, running the washcloth gently over her abused flesh.

"I didn't feel so much as a twinge when we made love."

Geni twisted, looking over her shoulder to take in as much as she could see of the bruising, already assuming alarmingly vibrant purple and black hues.

"I think it's all from getting bounced around in the back of that ute. I was lying on bare metal. But it's only bruising. I'll probably be stiff as a board tomorrow, but when I think of what might have happened, a few bruises are a small price."

Her voice rose, exultant, as she realised what Nigel Blount's death meant for her.

"Ben, I don't have to worry and feel frightened any longer. I'm free. Free." She did a rather cramped happy dance. The shower cubicle wasn't built for two.

Laughing, they quickly soaped and rinsed each other, then towelled each other dry. Geni dashed back into the bedroom to scramble into jeans and a long-sleeved shirt which would hide most of the livid bruises. Turning round, she saw Ben standing in the doorway, a towel wrapped around his waist,

"Hurry up and get dressed. We have to go in a few minutes."

"Small problem with that."

Wrinkling his nose in disgust, he bent down and picked up his dirty, wet overalls. "Not sure I can bear to put these on again until they've been laundered."

"Where did you leave your other clothes?"

"Last I saw they were on the back seat of the SES truck. I vaguely recall folding them up and stowing them in my kitbag. I wonder what Alan did with all my stuff?"

"I'll go and look, if you like," Geni volunteered, stifling a giggle. She could imagine the gossip if Ben was seen leaving her flat wearing nothing more than a towel. Without waiting for his answer, she jogged over to the door, opening it a crack to check that the coast was clear; and laughed out loud.

"Problem solved, Darling." She leaned out and picked up the kitbag sitting on the doormat, Ben's highly polished brown lace-ups placed neatly side by side on top of it.

"Alan must have brought this up when he put the truck away." She giggled.

"I wonder if he knocked. Do you know if we were being noisy? I bet he'll be taking the mickey out of us both next time we see him."

"As to that, I don't care." Ben's voice was muffled as he hauled his polo shirt over his head. "I told you that when your problems were sorted, I'd be asking you to marry me. I'm asking now." He went down on his knee at her feet. Holding her hand in his, he looked up at her.

"I love you Geni Sullivan. I'll love you forever. Will you do me the honour of becoming my wife?" He held his breath, waiting for her reply.

She didn't keep him waiting. Not even for one second, although it felt like a lifetime to Ben.

"Yes! Oh Ben, I love you too. And I'll love you forever, too." She pulled him to his feet, laughing and kissing him, until she remembered they didn't have time to celebrate the way she wanted to. Her son would be waiting impatiently for her to collect him from school.

~~~~~

They made it on time. Just. Ben pulled into his reserved space in the staff carpark as the bell sounded the end of the day.

Geni begged Ben to let her tell Jamie about her day's adventures herself, but asked him to join them for dinner so they could share their other, even happier, news together.

"I've got a better idea. I'll take you both to dinner at the pub to celebrate. Let Marge Morris do the cooking. You need to have that rest Eddie prescribed."

"The one you didn't give me time for?"

They laughed, both more than happy with the way they'd spent their afternoon. "Dinner out is a wonderful idea. And Jamie and I will walk home today. You probably have a heap of things you need to catch up on, Ben. One way or another, I've taken up your whole day."

"Time well spent, I assure you." He smiled, dipping his head for a quick kiss. To Hell with being seen and stirring up gossip. They were getting married! Everyone in town would know they were engaged pretty soon. He felt like dancing a jig, but that really would set tongues wagging. They'd probably clap him in a straitjacket. Instead, he kissed her again, taking his time over the thoroughly enjoyable task. Better than prancing about like an idiot.

Geni, her face one huge smile, gazed adorningly into his eyes as she slowly disentangled herself from his arms.

"We'll see you later. Oh Darling, it's so wonderful to feel safe, doing ordinary things like everyone else."

Geni, with fewer inhibitions than her lover, did a happy dance, wondering idly why it made Ben laugh so hard. She didn't care. She was walking on air, and he could laugh as hard as he liked.

With a flutter of her fingers, she jogged off to collect Jamie from outside Ms Marsden's office.

The first thing she did when she saw her son, was to drop her bag on the floor and sweep him up in an enthusiastic hug that elicited an embarrassed,

"Aw, Mu-um!"

Geni laughed again. He could protest all he liked, but she'd claim as many hugs and kisses as she wanted. Today was the most wonderful day of her life, and she felt the need to share her joy. After a few reassuring words, she thought of another thing which would please her son and hugged him again.

"You can even go out to play now, without an adult to watch over you every minute, Jamie, Love."

"Thanks Mum." He hugged her back. "Can I phone Bailey to tell him? I already told him about today, but he reckoned you'd need me to stay home and look after you. I'll stay home if you want me to," he offered with heroic generosity, making Geni laugh again.

"Not necessary, Love. I feel fine. Just a bit tired. Better than phoning Bailey, come on home now. Get changed, have a snack to sustain you till dinnertime, then you can go off and surprise him."

Jamie's answering whoop reminded her she wasn't the only one who'd felt like a prisoner recently. Until they were released from the threat hanging over them, she hadn't realised how very heavily it had weighed on her, dictating her every move. Freedom was a heady champagne bubbling through her veins. And when love was added to the mix... well, she almost felt she could fly.

~~~~~

Of course, Jamie couldn't keep good news to himself.

As soon as they arrived at The Victoria Inn, he told everyone his mum and Mr Wright were getting married. The waitress who took their orders.

Marge Morris who popped out of the kitchen to assure herself Geni was none the worse for her adventures; and then Phil Morris who stepped through from the bar, a frosted bottle of champagne in one hand and a pair of flutes in the other to congratulate Ben on his part in Geni's rescue. By then the whole pub was buzzing and a crowd was gathering to offer congratulations.

"Maybe eating out wasn't such a good idea," Geni, cheeks pink and eyes sparkling, laughed. "I better make a few phone calls or Megan will be thumping me next."

She dug her phone out from the bottom of her bag to phone Megan. And Angie. And Elizabeth. By which time Eddie and Mike Patterson were coming through the door into the dining room, followed within minutes by the rest of their friends. The contingent from 'Morgan's Run', including Alan's parents and daughters, were last to arrive, but only because they had the furthest to travel. What had started out as a quiet family dinner had ballooned into a whole community celebration. Even Don Matthews and his constables arrived to claim their share of hearty backslaps and bubbly.

Half-way through the evening, Geni felt a tug on her shirt-tail. Looking down she saw Jamie, his anxious face screwed up with worry.

"What's wrong, Love?"

She crouched down to talk to him eye-to-eye.

"You didn't do it just because I said I'd like it if Mr Wright was my father, did you?" he whispered, so no-one could overhear.

"No way, Mate." Geni, still exuberantly free with her hugs, pulled him close. "I'm glad you approve of him," she whispered back, "but I'm marrying him for me, Idiot." She ruffled his hair, then, leaning real close, she added, "I love him, Jamie. I really do. And he loves me. That's why we're getting married. You're included too, you know. The three of us are going to be a family."

"Okay, then." Relieved, he ran off back to where the children had gathered in their usual noisy pack.

16

Three weeks later Oxley Crossing celebrated again.

Late Friday afternoon, Megan's waters broke. She been prowling restlessly all day, unable to settle to anything. Wanting company, she'd descended on Geni, downstairs in the office, perching on the corner of her desk whenever there were no clients present, driving Geni to distraction while she wrestled with her interminable paperwork. In desperation, Geni had sent her to put the kettle on. Hearing her friend call out, Geni dropped everything and ran, imagining Megan had spilt hot tea on herself.

"It's the baby! It's coming!" Excitement tinged with panic met Geni when she skidded to a halt in the doorway. "What'll I do, Geni?"

"Sit down." Geni steered her into a chair. "Call Jon. Where's your phone?'

"Here." Megan pulled it out of her pocket, and Geni recalled seeing her using it several times that day, when she herself had been too busy to entertain her friend.

"Okay. Phone Jon, and I'll run upstairs and get you some fresh clothes." She gestured towards Megan's wet shorts. "Don't worry about the floor, I'll take care of it when I get back."

After that it was uncontrolled chaos as Jon and Mike came running from next door, offering conflicting advice, all of which Megan, concentrating on her first serious contraction, ignored.

Eddie, abandoning the library to her assistant, bustled in, and within minutes had restored order. Minutes later, Geni leaned through the open door of the car, kissed her friend on the cheek and wished her luck, then stepped back as Jon drove off, taking his wife to the local hospital where Doc Rogers and the midwife would shortly join them.

"We should all have a cup of tea, then go back to work," Eddie declared, wiping a stray tear from her eye. Usually on top of everything, she was unexpectedly dithery. Being childless herself, this was as close to a birth as she'd ever been, and she didn't know what was permissible. "It's bound to take ages, and we'll be no use to anyone."

"Nonsense!" Mike was made of sterner stuff. "We'll be there for our Meggie and Jon, however long it takes." He swept Eddie off to collect his own car.

Left to her own devices, Geni did a little more phoning, tidied up the office, and locked up. Outside, she went across to the park to find Jamie.

"Megan's having her baby," she explained. "I'm going to the hospital to wait. Bailey's mother said you can spend the night at their house."

~~~~~

Half an hour later, Ben strode into the hospital waiting room, going immediately to his fiancée's side.

"Any news yet?"

"Too soon. Doc Rogers says it's all going well, but he isn't guessing how long it'll be."

An hour later Alan and Angie joined them, asking the same questions and receiving the same answers. As seemed usual the women gravitated together on one side of the room and the men on the other. When delivering coffee from the urn in the corner, Geni overheard enough before Alan hushed the other two to realise they were taking bets on the time of birth, and the sex of the baby, since Megan had insisted on it being a good, old-fashioned surprise.

She grinned to herself, and, sidling alongside Ben, whispered, "What's your money on?" Caught out, he blushed, thought better of prevaricating, and leaned down to whisper in her ear.

"Midnight, and a boy for me. Two am and a girl for Mike, and five am and a boy for Alan. Don't tell Eddie, will you?"

Geni smirked. No, she wouldn't tell Eddie. And she wouldn't tell Ben that the ladies had their own little lottery going. They needed something to distract them during what was shaping up to be a long night.

Conversation became desultory, more than one person smothering a yawn as time went by with no further news from the delivery room. Ben fetched another round of hot drinks, and they all gravitated back together again.

"By the way," Alan took a sip of his fresh coffee, then finished his sentence. "I was talking to Pete Hackett earlier. He told me he's sold the old Murchison place across the creek. Some bloke by the name of Marten."

"That's right, Alan." Eddie, with more information to share on the subject, perked up. "Joshua Marten. I looked him up on-line. He's quite well-known in artistic circles as a sculptor. He won some big art prize a couple of years back."

"Wonder what he's coming here for? The Murchison place is falling down. No-one's lived there for years."

"No idea, Mike. Maybe he'll tear it down and rebuild. Besides, aren't you one of The Crossing's advocates? Perhaps he's looking for a tree-change." Angie laughed. "After all, you know, it's what I did; and I've never looked back."

She snuggled against Alan's side, and he dropped a quick kiss on the top of her head.

Just then, Jon, popping in briefly for a coffee, provided an update and Oxley Crossing's newest resident was forgotten.

"Fully dilated and she's in third stage labour," he said, then a harried expression on his face, he rushed back to Megan's side.

That was the last they heard until, shortly after twelve-thirty am, Doc Rogers stepped into the room.

"All done, people," he announced.

"Meggie was very considerate and got on with the job nice and efficiently. Baby arrived fifteen minutes ago. A girl. Pretty little thing, as babies go."

He grinned at the cheers and headed for the exit.

"Nurse Watkins is in charge. Either she or Jon can fill you in on the rest. I'm off to my bed. Goodnight."

It wasn't long till Jon appeared, beaming and slightly dazed. "I got chucked out while Megan's getting cleaned up and moved to her room. Did you hear? Megan's fine. We've got a baby girl! How about that Gran and Pop?" He hugged Eddie and Mike and tolerated the noisy congratulations for a bit then muttered, "Shut up a bit, you lot. I want to ring Dad. Tell him he's a grandfather."

~~~~~

They were allowed five minutes each with Megan, and a peep at the sleeping baby through the viewing window, then the hospital staff kicked them out.

It was while they were having their turn at the viewing window, that Ben, standing behind Geni with both arms wrapped around her, whispered in her ear.

"She's perfect, isn't she? I don't suppose…" When Geni looked at him over her shoulder, she was surprised at his wistful expression.

"Don't suppose what?" she whispered back.

"Do you reckon we could have one too? Doesn't have to be a girl. I'll be just as happy with a boy. You do want more than Jamie, don't you?"

Geni turned in his arms, reaching up to hold his face between both her hands.

"I most certainly do," she assured him, smiling as the faint frown lines smoothed out on his forehead. "In fact," she smiled seraphically, "we'll be having one sooner than we thought." She almost laughed out loud when his mouth dropped open and he gulped.

"But... I thought we were being careful?"

"We were. Only there was one memorable afternoon three weeks ago, when we both forgot all about being careful, didn't we?"

Ben picked her up and swung her round and round, only just remembering not to shout in the hospital corridor.

"What are you two on about?" They hadn't noticed the Morgans exit Megan's room, and the question took them by surprise.

"We're having one too. Isn't that fantastic!" Ben didn't stop to think. He simply blurted it out.

"Must be catching," Alan muttered, a grin on his face as he slapped Ben on the back.

"Does he mean...?" Geni turned to face Angie, her lips spread in a wide, quizzical grin. Angie nodded, an answering grin of her own on her face.

"Men!" she exclaimed softly. "They just can't keep a secret for five minutes, can they."

Epilogue

Angie checked that the flowergirls, Melanie and Jocelyn, were ready and knew what they had to do, helped Megan spread Geni's Chantilly lace train and billowing full-length veil just so, then walked to her place on the bride's side of the church and sat next to her husband.

He took her hand in his, and they looked to the altar where Ben, Jamie and Ben's brother, Justin Wright, were taking their places in front of Reverend Charles.

As the music swelled into a triumphal bridal march, Ben, nervously fingering a collar which suddenly felt too tight, turned expectantly.

Right on cue, Jocelyn, wearing a fairy princess gown in her favourite lavender, a matching floral wreath crowning her flowing dark curls, paced sedately down the exact centre of the aisle, nervously clutching her basket of flowers. She glanced sideways seeking her mother's approval. Receiving a proud smile and nod from Angie, she faced front again and stepped out more confidently.

Melanie, similarly gowned in palest gold with sunny yellow flowers adorning her tawny lion's mane, silently counted the beat. On precisely the correct note, she followed her sister. Head high, looking to neither right nor left, she made her entry a regal procession.

Alan, beaming proudly, squeezed Angie's hand. His parents, sitting on his far side, sighed audibly.

"Look, Poppet!" Whispered Eddie, standing to the side of the small church rocking tiny Chloe Armitage in her arms.

"Here comes your Mummy. Doesn't she look lovely?"

Sure enough, Megan was already half-way down the short aisle, apricot silk skimming lightly over a figure not yet back to its usual svelte lines so soon after Chloe's birth.

The music changed, and a concerted "Ooh," whispered through the nave as Geni entered on Mike Patterson's arm, a vision in lightly swathed silk and lace. If the girls were fairy princesses, then Geni was undoubtedly their queen. Titania in the flesh. Smiling radiantly, she had eyes for no-one except the man and boy waiting for her at the altar.

Ben relaxed, the tension visibly draining from too-tight shoulders.

He took a half-step forward, his hand lifted towards his bride, his smile as radiant as hers. His eyes fixed as intently on her as hers were on him. The love they had for each other warmed the hearts of everyone present to witness the wedding of Geni Sullivan to Benedict Wright.

~~~~~

The servers were clearing away the debris of the main course when Alan rose to his feet and tapped a spoon against his glass, signalling for quiet.

"Ladies and gentlemen, I'd like to propose a toast..." he began. The toast to the bride and groom was quickly followed by the rest of the customary wedding speeches and toasts, then, with the servers hovering in the wings, waiting to bring in the desserts, Alan once again took the floor.

"Last speech, I promise," he grinned. "I know you're all starving and want to get on with the important part of the meal, but there's one more very special speech. Jamie..." He turned, gesturing with his arm for the boy to rise.

"Um, I. I..." Jamie stuttered nervously into the microphone he'd been handed.

He'd asked Uncle Alan if he could do this, but now the moment had arrived, he'd been attacked by stage-fright, all his carefully rehearsed words erased from his mind. Humiliated, he felt tears threatening.

Desperately, he searched the auditorium, finally catching sight of his mate, Bailey Tan. A mile-wide grin on his face, Bailey was giving him a big thumbs-up sign. With his mate's support, Jamie's courage flowed back, along with the words he thought he'd forgotten. He straightened, drew a deep breath, and started again.

"I've never had a Dad before, but I just know the one I got today is going to be terrific." He looked across his mother's head to his newly acquired parent.

"Dad, you asked me to be your best man today, and I want to tell you in front of all our family and friends, that you will always be my best man. I love you Dad, and I'm so happy you married Mum."

Blushing furiously, he sat abruptly. Congratulatory whistling and clapping broke out, their guests rising to their feet. At the top table, Jamie was in the middle of a sandwich hug, caught between his mother and his brand-new father.

Two hours later Ben and Geni were about ready to make their escape. Just as soon as they performed their final duties. Ben went down on one knee to ceremoniously remove Geni's garter, serenaded by whistles and catcalls. With a wink at the handful of young bachelors, he turned his back and tossed it over his shoulder.

Amid laughter and shouts of, "Mine!", and "No, I've got it.", during which Joey Lambert and Charlie Molinar almost came to blows, the blue satin garter bounced from hand to hand, finally coming to rest with Bob Whitman, who stood there staring at it clenched in his fist with a stunned-mullet look of horror on his face. He slunk off to the back of the crowd, away from the back-slapping and chiacking.

Then it was Geni's turn. When she tossed the bouquet, it was touched by only one pair of hands. Sophie James, the tallest of the bevy of single girls reached up, plucking it from the air as it sailed over their heads.

Bob had looked put out at his luck. Not so Sophie. She looked as smug as a cat on a sunny window sill.

Especially so for a girl who didn't even have a boyfriend.

More than one of the older ladies commented on the fact that Sophie and Bob had had their heads together for most of the reception. They reckoned the pair of them bore watching in the future.

THE END

I hope you enjoyed reading

Finding Mr Wright.

Please turn the page for a preview of Lena West's new Oxley Crossing Romance, *Electing Robert Whitman.*

Here is Your Preview of
Electing Robert Whitman

An Oxley Crossing Romance, Book 4 in the series

LENA WEST

Love in Oxley Crossing
Australian Rural Romance
4

Electing Robert Whitman

LENA WEST

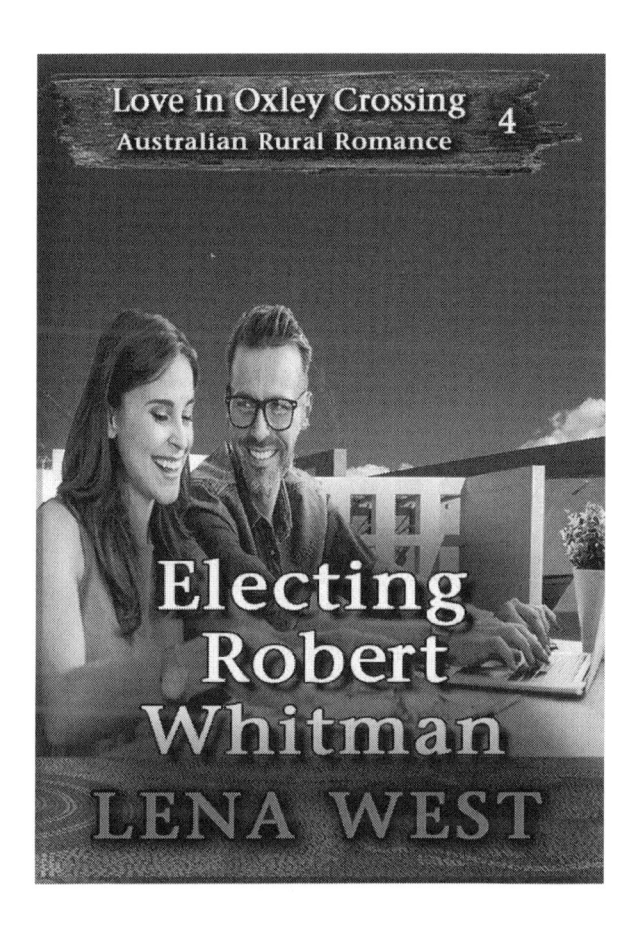

FINDING MR WRIGHT

1

Something good was about to happen.

She could 'feel it in her water' as Gran used to say. Maybe she'd meet the man she was destined to fall in love with. She was at a wedding, after all, with romance casting its aura far and wide, so that was not an unreasonable assumption.

Anticipation humming through her veins lent added sparkle to Sophie James's warm, brown eyes as, stopping frequently to exchange greetings, she strolled between the tables in the main auditorium of the Oxley Crossing Bowling Club, searching for the place card bearing her name. She had expected to be on the same table as her mother, whose invited partner she was at this wedding. But while her mother was happily seated at a table of older people, several of whom were ranked among her particular cronies, she herself was still looking for her seat.

She was lucky to be able to attend, as she wasn't often in The Crossing, now she was working full time in Port Macquarie.

When her mother had invited her to be the 'and partner' on her invitation, she had jumped at the chance of a night out with the old crowd. That alone was reason enough for her upbeat mood, but she was certain the tingle in her blood signified something of far more importance than a simple good night out with friends. If that was all it took to get her feeling like this, she'd be tingling madly every other time she poked her nose out the door.

Even though she didn't know either Geni Sullivan or Ben Wright particularly well, she liked them both and was happy to be celebrating with them tonight. Theirs had been a dramatic, whirlwind romance which almost came to grief when Geni's violent ex-husband had kidnapped her. The event, with its tragic outcome for Nigel Blount, Geni's ex, had been the talk of The Crossing ever since, although the recent birth of the Armitage baby had almost toppled it from top spot.

"Hey Sophie," she looked up as Joey Lambert whistled and called out to attract her attention. "You're over here with us. Looks like this table was reserved for young singles."

Well, that makes sense, Sophie thought.

Smiling, she made her way to join Joey and the handful of other young people, all of whom she had gone to school with several years earlier. Good friends all of them. Some better than others, she thought, spotting her one-time BFF, Pam Lanner approaching. Knowing everyone was one of the advantages of growing up in a small town. It was also one of the disadvantages; since there was always someone who knew where the dirt was buried. There were no secrets in a small town, something newcomers often failed to realise until too late.

Being a total stranger in the regional city of Port Macquarie, she was still somewhat ambivalent about the anonymity of her position there. Not that she'd have to be concerned about it for much longer.

Her plum job had been as a temporary replacement for a woman on extended maternity leave, who now wanted her job back. Not unexpected, but Sophie had been hoping the new mum would be so enamoured with motherhood she'd choose to stay away a while longer. Long enough for *her* to really impress the boss with her valuable contribution to the company, and maybe be offered a permanent position of her own.

Sophie had told her mother over breakfast. She wasn't looking forward to joining the multitude of aspiring hopefuls all with their ambitions pinned on the rare vacancies in the most prestigious companies, but Dorothy, her mother, had had serious news of her own. Only half attending to the disjointed conversation going on around her, Sophie ran the breakfast conversation through her mind once again.

"Sophie dear," her mother had begun, "I have to go into hospital for a little op. My old trouble," she had waved off Sophie's instinctive exclamations. "The difference is, this time the doctors say I need the op or it will just get worse, and then I might be in real trouble."

"I'll be there at the hospital with you, Mum,"

Sophie reached out to clasp her mother's hand, offering tacit comfort.

"Off course you will, Dear." Her mother patted her hand.

"It's just, hearing your news, I had the idea you might be able to help me out with another small problem, since you'll be out of work for a little bit right at the time I need someone. It seemed providential, but don't think you have to agree if something comes up for you in the meantime. I know how important your career is to you," her mother had finished up, half apologetically.

A couple more questions had elicited the whole story. Her mother's full-time assistant in her shop, the Oxley Crossing Newsagent, an experienced woman more than capable of taking over in an emergency, was on holiday. She had taken three months leave and gone to visit family in England. The other assistants, all part-timers, were willing workers, but none of them able to run the business.

"You'd like me to step up and hold the fort till you're back on your feet," Sophie had broken in, cutting off her mother's guilty rambling explanation. "In that case, it really is providential, my being free just when you need me. I'll defer looking for a new job until you're able to take over again."

It wasn't what Sophie had been planning for her immediate future, but her mother had always been there for her, and now the boot was on the other foot, she was happy to fill in. The relief on her mother's face confirmed the rightness of her snap decision.

Sophie kissed cheeks and exchanged greetings, rather surprised to find herself still dwelling on the subject of her employment. It wasn't as if working in her mother's shop was anything new. She'd spent most of her holidays as a student working for her mother to supplement her student allowance.

The MC, Alan Morgan, began shepherding everyone to their tables, as the bridal party was about to make their entrance.

Sophie walked round the table to her spot; and had one of those *déjà vu* moments.

Her table partner was Robert Whitman. Again. Just as he had been at the last wedding she'd attended. Megan Patterson's wedding. Sophie laughed silently to herself, willing to bet Eddie Paterson had been responsible both times. Eddie and her propensity for matchmaking were legendary in The Crossing. *Successful matchmaking*, Sophie amended, her heart skipping a beat.

After meeting Robert for the first time in ages, she'd hoped he would follow up on what had been a very enjoyable evening. She supposed it wasn't surprising he hadn't, since they lived in different parts of the country, but she'd felt disappointed, nonetheless.

Was this second meeting, an apparent reprise on the last, what was setting off the tingles? Did she want a second chance to attract Robert Whitman's attention? And then the man himself was there, seating her politely like the gentleman he indisputably was. His hand rested momentarily on her shoulder, and her pulse kicked into a higher gear.

"Sophie. I didn't know you were home. It's good to see you again." He actually did sound pleased, Sophie noted. Thus encouraged, she impulsively decided to try her luck with him.

Robert Whitman, whom most people referred to as Bob, wasn't every girl's dream man. *All the better for me*, Sophie concluded, regarding him with a critical eye.

Less competition.

The glasses he wore made him appear a bit nerdish. Coupled with his punctilious dress code and a tendency to pontificate when he got on his hobbyhorse, he'd been the butt of a few unkind jokes at school. But Sophie liked a well-dressed man, and she shared a number of his interests. They'd always had plenty to talk about.

Sophie had always looked below the surface with Robert, and she didn't believe he would have changed fundamentally. She saw a, dark haired, pleasant featured man who was borderline handsome; not particularly tall, but still comfortably taller than herself. Appraising him objectively, she came to the conclusion he would become distinguished looking with the addition of a few more years. He cared passionately about his family, his country and his community; in that order. Sentiments with which she agreed wholeheartedly.

Sophie liked Robert Whitman. A lot. She always had, ever since the time he'd come to the rescue, when, a timid five-year old, she'd been teased at school. A high school boy at the time, his support had carried weight among her much younger classmates. After that, he'd made a point of seeing she was okay until it became obvious she'd found her feet, although he'd continued to wave or call a greeting in passing. He still did.

Little Sophie had adored her champion from afar. Years later, teenage Sophie had met him on one of his visits home from university, and the adoration had developed into a full-blown crush which she had never entirely outgrown. Adult Sophie wondered if a closer relationship might be possible now the age divide between them had narrowed to acceptability.

"It's good to see you, too, Robert," she responded with an almost intimate smile. "I miss my friends so much when I'm away."

There was no time for more until the servers began circulating with the entrees, and even then, it was general, with the conversation being batted back and forth around the table as everyone caught up on the latest happenings. Sophie bided her time until attention turned mainly to food.

Robert wasn't sure sitting next to little Sophie James was a particularly good idea. He'd always found her way too attractive for comfort. Considering the age gap between them, he'd felt the attraction to be inappropriate, and had hoped it would disappear, aided by time and distance. It hadn't.

Last year she'd about knocked him for six when they ended up together at Megan's wedding. Just as well she'd gone back to Port Macquarie. Out of sight, but unfortunately, not out of mind. Now he had to cope with her all over again, and the worst of it was, one glance had been enough for him to know it would be harder to resist her this time.

"Last time we met, Robert, you were telling me you planned to enter the political arena. Is that still your goal?"

"It is, Soph."

Politics. Robert clutched at the lifeline he'd been thrown. If he could keep the conversation safely centred on his future career, he might just make it through the meal without giving himself away.

"I'm working in Arthur Steedman's office. Our Federal Member of Parliament, you know."

Robert informed her.

"He's an Independent, which is what I want to be, and he's grooming me to stand at the next State election in just over a year's time. He reckons I'll be ready by then."

"How wonderful! I think you'll be an excellent rep for this electorate." Sophie chuckled, causing a raised eyebrow. "It just occurred to me, I can come knocking on your door, once you've won your seat, to ask for a recommendation for a back-room job. I'm in public relations, and I'd love to work in the House."

Robert preened guiltily. He wasn't accustomed to admiration from attractive young women, but little Sophie James wasn't like the other girls. Sophie looked up to him, which made it damned difficult remembering not to step out of line with her. Although, she was not so little now. He cast a surreptitious, yet extremely comprehensive eye over her stylishly clad figure, confirming what had disconcerted him so much the year before.

Sophie James had grown up very nicely indeed, with glossy, dark brown hair tumbling smoothly over her shoulders and enticing curves in all the right places. He felt his body responding to her presence, and adjusted his position slightly, giving thanks his dignity was preserved by the table cloth.

It was enough to make him wish he wasn't so much older than her. A young woman like Sophie wouldn't look twice at a man of his age with so many options among her own age group. A sweep of the table, noting the several handsome young men present, was sufficient to depress any pretensions he might have.

If that wasn't enough, there was a city full of eligible young blokes down in Port Macquarie. Imagining Sophie in another man's arms gave him a bad few moments. But she was still talking. He tuned back in to her conversation.

"I noticed the new look, Robert. I like it. The designer stubble makes you stand out in a crowd. Was it your girlfriend's idea?" The last bit was added so she could find out his current status without giving herself away by asking an outright question.

"Thanks. I think. It was accidental really. I was running late one morning and didn't have time to shave. Mrs Steedman approved of the new look and suggested I cultivate it." He remembered Sophie's tail-end question, debating whether or not to ignore it. He shrugged mentally. If she didn't hear it from him, someone else would probably fill her in, and really, it didn't matter, did it?

"No girlfriend. I seem to be plagued with the worst luck when it comes to romance." He grimaced. "Mum tells me to stop worrying about it. She reckons I'll know the right woman when I see her, then everything will be smelling of roses."

"She's undoubtedly right." Sophie placidly reverted to discussing his political career, but inside she gave a mental air pump. Robert Whitman was still single and available. If that wasn't providence giving her a nudge, she didn't know what was. She didn't know whether her attraction to him would grow into love, but it was stronger than anything she'd felt for the handful of boyfriends she'd had in the past. Relationships which had all fizzled out to nothing. She decided to make the most of her heaven-sent return to The Crossing and explore the possibilities.

"You know, Robert," she leaned closer so he could hear her above the rising noise level, "I'm going to be home for a bit. Mum has to go into hospital in a fortnight, and I'm helping her out in the shop for a few weeks. I'll have plenty of time on my hands, so how would you like it if I helped you get your campaign off the ground?" He looked startled by her suggestion, and she jumped in quickly before he could refuse her help.

"I told you I'd like a job in the House. Working on your campaign would look good on my CV, so how about it?"

~~~~~

Before they left the table, Sophie had wrung a firm agreement from Robert. As soon as she returned to The Crossing in two weeks, she would be working with him in the evenings to plan the most effective political campaign the region had ever seen. The work would be satisfying, career wise, and as for romance... Surely propinquity would reveal her true feelings, and Robert's, to her, one way or the other. Although if the one dance she'd managed to snaffle with him was any indication, their prospects were promising. As long as the fireworks had been mutual; which, considering he had made no effort to monopolise her during the remainder of the evening, was yet to be determined.

Continued...

Get

"Electing Robert Whitman"

as soon as it's released. Go to

www.lenawestauthor.com

and make sure you are signed up for news and release notices!

About the Author

Born in tropical North Queensland, Lena loves living close to the sea, although she moved frequently during her early years, living everywhere from large cities to isolated farms. Her most recent home has a deck overlooking the ocean, which is her favourite room in the house, for reading, writing, art, craft or even birdwatching, when the local birds come to visit.

After working as a primary school teacher in both her native Queensland, and later in New South Wales where she met her own romantic hero, she took a very early retirement to travel Australia with him, in a motorhome. This idyllic lifestyle lasted several years, during which time she indulged in the creation of story plots and their settings, culminating in her taking steps to fulfil her lifelong ambition to write.

Storytelling came naturally - she had been making up stories for her own entertainment all her life, but it wasn't until she began traveling that she had time to write down some of her favourites. Now published, *Marrying Alan Morgan*, is the first in a series of rural romances set in the fictional town of Oxley Crossing.

It is followed by the second in the series, *Saving Jonathon Armitage* and the third, *Finding Mr Wright* with several more in the series planned. She also writes standalone contemporary romances, of which *Loving Fenella* has been released. An Australian historical romance, *Unto Death,* will be released soon.

Lena has an addiction to happily-ever-afters, in both her reading and her own stories, so the romance genre was a natural fit, and the variety of places she has lived have all added to the settings in which she brings love to life.

You can find Lena on Facebook at:

https://www.facebook.com/LenaWestAuthor/

or sign up for her newsletter at :

www.lenawestauthor.com

Other Books by Lena West

Standalone Contemporary Romances

Loving Fenella

https://www.amazon.com/dp/B07B3RLS98/

Bronwyn's Family (Coming soon)

Contemporary Series

Love in Oxley Crossing Series

Marrying Alan Morgan

https://www.amazon.com/dp/B0774V1L25/

Saving Jonathon Armitage

https://www.amazon.com/dp/B0788GCQJQ

Finding Mr Wright

Electing Robert Whitman (Coming 2018)

Redeeming Josh Marten (Coming soon)

The Making of Joey Lambert (Coming soon)

The Wyldeflower Series

(Coming soon)

Historical Romances

Unto Death (May 2018)

Emily's baby (Coming soon)

Home is the Heart (Coming soon)

Blue Streak (Coming soon)

Love and War (Coming soon

Connect with Lena!

Be the first to know about it when Lena's next book is released!

Sign up to Lena's newsletter at

www.lenawestauthor.com

Printed in Great Britain
by Amazon